REAWAKENED BY THE SURGEON'S TOUCH

BY
JENNIFER TAYLOR

MILLS BOON

First published in Great Britain 2016
By Mills & Boon, an imprint of HarperCollins*Publishers*
1 London Bridge Street, London, SE1 9GF

Large Print edition 2017

© 2016 Jennifer Taylor

ISBN: 978-0-263-06693-7

Printed and bound in Great Britain
by CPI Antony Rowe, Chippenham, Wiltshire

Jennifer Taylor has written for several different Mills & Boon series, but it wasn't until she 'discovered' Medical Romances that she found her true niche. Jennifer loves the blend of modern romance and exciting medical drama. Widowed, she divides her time between homes in Lancashire and the Lake District. Her hobbies include reading, walking, travelling and spending time with her two gorgeous grandchildren.

Books by Jennifer Taylor

Mills & Boon Medical Romance

The Family Who Made Him Whole
The Son that Changed His Life
The Rebel Who Loved Her
The Motherhood Mix-Up
Mr Right All Along
Saving His Little Miracle
One More Night with Her Desert Prince...
Best Friend to Perfect Bride
Miracle Under the Mistletoe
The Greek Doctor's Secret Son

Visit the Author Profile page
at millsandboon.co.uk for more titles.

In memory of Jean and Bob Taylor.
The best parents anyone could have had.

Praise for
Jennifer Taylor

'A superbly written tale of hope, redemption and forgiveness, *The Son that Changed His Life* is a first-class contemporary romance that plumbs deep into the heart of the human spirit and touches the soul.'

—CataRomance

'Powerful, compassionate and poignant, *The Son that Changed His Life* is a brilliant read from an outstanding writer who always delivers!'

—CataRomance

CHAPTER ONE

WHAT IN HEAVEN'S name was he doing here?

As the plane began the final stages of its descent, Jude Slater was struck by an unexpected rush of panic. Up to this point anger had buoyed him up. He had been so furious when his former mentor, a man he greatly admired, had accused him of choosing the easy option that he had set out to prove him wrong. Maybe it wouldn't have stung quite so much if Jude hadn't had the sneaking suspicion that the other man was right. He *had* been coasting for the past few years, although he had refused to justify himself by explaining why. He tried not to think about that period in his life; it was too painful. Suffice to say that he had paid his dues, even if it didn't appear so to an outsider.

Nevertheless, the accusation had spurred him

on so that almost before he knew it, he had signed up to work for Worlds Together, a leading medical aid agency. True, he had been a little disconcerted when he had been invited for an interview a couple of weeks later and offered a post. He hadn't expected things to move quite so quickly but he had been determined not to back down. Nobody would be able to accuse him of losing sight of the real issues once he had done a stint overseas, he had assured himself. He would be accorded his true standing within the medical fraternity and that was all he wanted. It had all sounded so perfect in theory but now that he was about to land in the tiny central African country of Mwuranda reality had set in.

What did he know about the problems of working in the developing world? Jude thought a shade desperately. He was London born and London bred, and he thrived in the constant bustle of city life. When he travelled abroad, he visited other cities—New York, Paris, Rome—places where he felt at home. Wherever he went, he stayed in five-star luxury hotels too; however, re-

calling what he had been told at his interview—
something about Mwuranda recovering from the
effects of civil war—it appeared that five-star
luxuries were going to be very thin on the ground
here!

The plane rumbled to a halt and Jude unfas-
tened his seat belt. Ten hours spent squeezed
into a gap between piles of packing cases hadn't
made for the most comfortable journey but, hopefully, things would improve from here on. The
one thing he mustn't do was panic. Conditions
couldn't be that bad or nobody would volunteer
to work here, so it was just a question of putting everything into perspective. Maybe luxuries
would be few and far between, but so long as he
had the basic necessities he would cope. He was
only here for three months and he could put up
with a bit of hardship for that length of time.

Jude felt much better once he had reasoned everything out. He had been told that he would be
collected from the airfield, so as soon as the ramp
was lowered, he made his way out of the plane.
His heart sank as he stepped onto the runway

and looked around. All he could see in every direction was khaki-coloured landscape, the few scrubby trees which were dotted about providing the only relief from the monotony. It was mid-afternoon and the air was blisteringly hot. Apart from the plane he had arrived on, the airfield was deserted. He couldn't see any sign of a car waiting to collect him and his spirits sank even further at the thought of having to hang around in the heat until his transport arrived.

'Dr Slater?'

The voice was female but that was the only indication of the speaker's gender, Jude discovered when he turned around. The figure standing before him was dressed in a bulky old boiler suit which completely disguised the wearer's shape. Heavy boots on her feet and an old baseball cap pulled low over her eyes completed her ensemble.

Jude could just make out the lower part of her face—a softly rounded chin and a mouth which was bare of any trace of lipstick. He had no idea if she was young, old or somewhere in between, and it was unsettling when it meant that he wasn't sure how to pitch his response.

'That's right. I'm Jude Slater.' He held out his hand and smiled charmingly at her. 'And you are—?'

'Your driver.'

The woman ignored his outstretched hand as she stared past him into the hold and Jude felt himself bridle. Quite frankly, he wasn't used to women of any age ignoring him. The older ones wanted to mother him, the younger ones wanted to sleep with him, while those in between could go either way.

'If you've brought any luggage with you then you'd better fetch it. There's a truck on its way to pick up our supplies, but there's no guarantee it will make it back to town tonight. It all depends how long it takes to unload the cargo.' The woman treated him to a cursory glance and he could tell how unimpressed she was by his attempts to charm her by the sneering curve of her unadorned lips. 'We don't drive around after dark. It's far too dangerous.' Jude's chagrin faded in the face of this fresh snippet of information. He managed to hide his dismay but the situation seemed to be going from bad to worse at a rate of knots.

'I'll get my bag,' he said shortly.

'You do that. I just need a word with the pilot and I'll be right with you. The bike's over there.'

Jude stopped dead, wondering if he had mis-heard her. It had been extremely noisy in the plane and his ears were still ringing from the throbbing of the engines, but he could have sworn she had said something about a... 'Bike?'

'Uh-huh.' She pointed across the runway. 'That's it over there. There's some rope under the seat, so I suggest you tie your bag onto the back. It should be safe enough so long as we don't hit too many potholes.'

Jude's jaw dropped when he spotted the bat-tered old motorbike propped against the perim-eter fence. Its bodywork was pitted with rust and even from this distance he could tell that the tyres were completely bald of any tread. She didn't *re-*

ally think that he was going to travel on the back of that thing, did she?

'This is a joke, isn't it? Some sort of a...*stunt* you pull on new recruits like me?' His good humour returned in a rush as he realised what was going on and he laughed. 'You wind us up by telling us that we're expected to ride on the back of that heap of junk and I, in my innocence, very nearly fell for it!'

'I hate to disillusion you, Dr Slater, but it isn't a wind-up. We'll be travelling back to town on that bike, so I suggest you get your belongings together.' The woman pushed back her cuff. 'It's almost two o'clock and I haven't got time to waste, hanging about here. If you don't want to spend the night sleeping in the plane then you'd better get a move on.'

With that she walked away. Jude watched her make her way over to where the crew were standing then realised that he was holding his breath. He breathed out and then in, but not even a fresh shot of oxygen made him feel any better. His gaze went to the rusty old motorbike and his mouth thinned. Given the choice, he would have refused to get on the blasted thing but he didn't have a choice, did he? He was a stranger in this country and one who knew very little about what it took to survive here too. He might be able to hold his own in any city in the world but he was as vulnerable as a newborn babe out here and it was galling to admit it.

He was used to running his life the way he chose these days. It had taken him a while to get back on track after he had quit working for the NHS and he had no intention of relinquishing his autonomy ever again. Maybe he was at a disadvantage here but he still intended to be in charge of his own destiny.

Jude took another deep breath and used it this time for a specific purpose, i.e. shoring up his anger. He would start as he meant to go on. No way was he going to be ordered about by some overbearing, pushy woman!

'I'm sorry about the delay but our usual driver didn't show up this morning and we had to find a replacement.' Claire Morgan glanced at her watch again and frowned. 'The truck should have been here by now, though, so I don't know what's happened to it. I'll have to check back with base and see if they've heard anything.'

She left the crew to begin the task of unloading the cargo and made her way over to the bike. Dr Slater had just finished roping his very expensive leather holdall onto the back and he looked round when he heard her approaching. Claire pulled the peak of her cap lower over her eyes, hating the fact that she felt it necessary to hide beneath it. She had hoped that she had got over this fear but as soon as she had seen Dr Jude Slater disembarking from the plane, her internal alarm bells had started ringing.

She knew what the problem was, of course: he reminded her of Andrew. There was something about that air of self-confidence he exuded that put her in mind of her ex so that it was an effort to carry on walking towards him. The thought of having to live with this fear gnawing away inside her for the next few months was more than she could bear, so maybe she needed to focus on the differences between the two men rather than the similarities?

It was worth a try, so Claire tested out the theory as she crossed the runway. Jude Slater was tall like Andrew, but whereas Andrew was heavily built, Jude had the lithely muscular physique of an athlete. Both men had dark hair, but Jude's hair was jet black with the hint of a wave to it whereas Andrew's was a rather muddy shade of brown and poker-straight. Jude's eyes were a different colour, too, Claire realised as she drew closer—a warm hazel with flecks of gold in them. Andrew's eyes were pale blue, very cold and frosty. In fact, if she had to choose one feature which she had disliked it would have been Andrew's eyes. Even when they had been sharing their most intimate moments, his eyes had never held any real warmth.

Claire sighed. With the benefit of hindsight, she could see that she should have taken it as a warning but she had been too besotted at the time to read the signs properly. It was a mistake she wouldn't make again. If she ever reached a point where she could consider having a relationship with a man again then she wouldn't choose someone who looked like Andrew or Jude Slater, for that matter.

'Is everything sorted out?'

'Nearly.' Claire's tone was clipped as she stopped beside the motorbike. She didn't look at him as she lifted the seat and took out the two-way radio transmitter. She had done her best—flagged up the differences—but it hadn't helped as much as she had hoped it would. She still had this deep-seated urge to run away and hide, and it was painful to acknowledge how little progress she had made in the past two years.

'Nearly? So do I take it there's a problem?' he persisted, obviously not satisfied with her less-than-fulsome reply.

Claire ignored him as she tuned the radio to the correct frequency. Although most of the rebel fighters had been driven out of the area, there were still pockets of resistance and keeping in touch with base was vital.

'Hello!' He stepped forward and bent to peer under the peak of her cap. 'I asked you a question. Did you hear me?'

Claire immediately recoiled. 'Do you mind,' she snapped, twisting the dial this way and that in the hope that it would disguise the fact that her hands were trembling. She hated it when anyone invaded her personal space. It was a trick Andrew had used to intimidate her and even though there was no reason to think that Jude Slater was trying to do the same, she resented it. Bitterly.

'I'm sorry. I just find it frustrating when people won't answer a simple question.'

He stepped back, folding his arms across his chest as he leant against the fence post, but Claire knew that he had sensed her discomfort. Colour ran up her face as she bent over the radio. Nobody knew about her past. Not even her family or her friends knew what she had been through. She had been too devastated to tell them the truth, that Andrew had forced her to have sex with him, that he had raped her. Women like her—intelligent, independent women—were supposed to be able to look after themselves. They weren't supposed to put themselves in a situation whereby something like that could happen. If they did then the consensus was that they were to blame for leading the man on.

It had taken Claire a long time to accept that she hadn't been at fault and that it was Andrew who was the guilty party. However, she knew how fragile her confidence was and there was no way that she was going to risk undoing all her hard work. Maybe Dr Slater wasn't cut from the same cloth but she wasn't going to test out *that* theory. For the next three months she intended to keep her distance from him and, more important, make sure he kept his distance from her.

'I need to contact base,' she explained as coolly as she could. 'The truck that was supposed to collect our supplies should have arrived by now and I need to find out what's happened to it.'

'It could have broken down en route.' Jude shrugged when she looked at him. 'If it's the same vintage as this machine then I'd say it's more than likely, wouldn't you?'

'It's possible. But I drove along the route the truck would have taken on my way here and I didn't see any sign of it—' She broke off when the radio crackled. The reception was terrible and she winced when a series of ear-splitting shrieks erupted from the handset. Twisting the dial, she tried to find a better signal, but it was no clearer.

'Here, let me have a go.'

He reached over and took the radio off her before she could object. He turned the dial the merest fraction and the next moment, Claire heard Lola's voice flowing across the airwaves. He handed the handset back to her with a smile that immediately set her teeth on edge. She knew it was silly to get upset over something so trivial, but his actions smacked of condescension and it was the one thing guaranteed to rile her.

Andrew had displayed the same high-handed attitude towards her. He had treated her with a mixture of charm and contempt from the moment they had met only she had been too naive to realise it. The way he had taken over at every opportunity had seemed touchingly gallant and she had enjoyed having him take care of her. It had taken her a while to realise that there was nothing gallant about his desire to rule her life, and definitely nothing gallant about the way he had reacted when she had told him that she no longer wanted to see him. Sickness roiled inside her at the memory and she forced it down. She had nothing to fear because she wasn't going to put herself in that position again.

'Thank you,' she said coldly, turning so that she could speak to Lola without having to look at Jude. 'Hi, Lola, it's me—Claire. I'm at the airfield and the truck hasn't arrived. Have you heard anything?'

'Not a word, hon. Give me a second and I'll see if I can get hold of the driver.'

Claire waited while Lola tried to contact Ezra, the truck driver. The heat was stifling that day and she could feel sweat trickling between her shoulder blades. The boiler suit she was wearing wasn't the most comfortable outfit in these conditions but all the women on the team made a point of covering themselves up whenever they left the hospital. Although the Mwurandans were lovely people on the whole, there had been a few unpleasant incidents recently, and it was safer to err on the side of caution.

'I can't raise him, Claire. I'll keep trying but at the moment I can't get a reply.'

Lola came back on the line. Claire frowned when she heard what the other woman said. 'Maybe his radio's down. Some of the sets are on their last legs, so that could be the problem.'

'Could be. Anyway, you'll be driving back along the same route, won't you, so you should pass him on the way.'

'I suppose so. Thanks, Lola.' Claire switched off the radio and stowed it under the seat then turned to Jude, trying not to let him see that she was concerned about what might have happened to the truck. 'We'd better make a move. There's no point hanging around here. The driver will just have to bed down in the plane if it's too late for him to drive back to town tonight.'

She straddled the scooter and started the engine then looked round when she realised that he hadn't moved. 'Are you coming or not?'

'Do I have a choice?' He sighed as he swung his leg over the seat. 'It's either a ride on this contraption or a night in the hold. Not much of a choice really, is it?'

'What did you expect? A chauffeur-driven limousine?' Claire retorted, letting out the clutch. The motorbike bucked as the gears engaged and she heard him swear as he grabbed hold of her around the waist.

'Do you have a licence for this thing?' he demanded, leaning forward so she could hear him above the roar of the engine.

Claire gripped the handlebars, her heart pounding as she felt the weight of his body pressing against her back. It had been a long time since she had been this close to a man and the memories it evoked weren't pleasant ones, either. It was all she could do to behave with apparent calm as they set off. 'No, I don't have a licence as it happens. However, I've not had an accident yet, so you should be safe enough.'

She increased their speed as they left the air-field, weaving her way around the potholes that peppered the road, and felt Jude's grip on her tighten.

'You really know how to reassure a guy, don't you?'

'I try,' Claire retorted.

She skirted around a particularly large hole, grinning to herself when she heard his breath hiss out as the rear wheel clipped the edge. Maybe it wasn't a kind thing to do but she had to admit that it felt good to be in control. She had a feeling that Jude Slater rarely allowed other people to order him about and she may as well make the most of it while she could. Once they were back at the hospital, she was going to do as she had said and steer well clear of him. It wouldn't be a hardship. From what she had seen so far, he was more trouble than he was worth!

CHAPTER TWO

THEY DROVE FOR almost a quarter of an hour in silence. Claire suspected that it was a combination of the noise from the engine plus a fear of her driving which was keeping Jude quiet, not that she was sorry, of course. When he suddenly leant forward she had to steel herself not to react as she felt the solid length of his body pressing against her back.

'What's that over there? Is it the missing truck?'

Claire slowed so that she could look at where he was pointing and felt her stomach sink when she spotted the truck partly hidden by some trees. All their vehicles were old and riddled with rust which was why the truck had blended so perfectly into the background; in fact, she wouldn't have noticed it if Jude hadn't pointed it out.

'It looks like it,' she agreed, bringing the motorbike to a halt at the side of the road. She kept the engine idling while she looked around, but there was no sign of movement from what she could see. The area appeared to be deserted, although she wasn't about to take that as proof there was nobody about. It could be a trap set by the rebel fighters and she needed to be on her guard. Switching off the engine, she climbed off the bike, nodding to Jude to indicate that he should get off as well. Opening the seat, she took out the pistol.

'You carry a *gun*?'

The shock in his voice would have been comical in other circumstances but not right then. Claire was starting to get a bad feeling about this and she didn't need him kicking up a fuss.

'This isn't Mayfair, Dr Slater. This is the middle of Africa and there are rebel factions active in the area.' She nodded at the bike. 'Stay here while I go and see what's happened.'

She didn't wait to check that he was following instructions. She just headed towards the truck, sure in her own mind that the handsome

Dr Slater would prefer not to risk his *oh-so-handsome* skin. Anyway, she needed to keep her wits about her instead of worrying about him…

'Shouldn't we find some cover? We're sitting ducks out here in the open.'

Claire spun round when she heard him hiss the question at her and glared at him. 'I thought I told you to stay with the bike!'

'You did,' he said shortly, staring past her. His hand shot out when she went to walk away. 'Wait! I thought I saw something move— Yes! There! Just to the left of the truck—did you see it?'

Claire screwed up her eyes against the glare from the sun as she stared towards the truck. 'I can't see anything.'

'It could have been a bird, I suppose.' He turned to her and she could tell from the set of his mouth that it would be a waste of time ordering him to go back to the bike. 'OK. Shall we do this, then?'

'Yes, but stay behind me.' She gave him a grim little smile. 'I wouldn't like you to get between me and any potential target.'

'And here was I thinking that you would love the chance to put a bullet in my back.'

He gave her a mocking smile then set off, ignoring her instructions as he led the way towards the trees. Claire muttered something uncomplimentary under her breath as she hurried after him. Why, for two pins, she would haul him straight back to the plane and have the crew lock him in the hold! Didn't he understand how dangerous the situation was and that they were both at risk of walking into a trap? Yet he had to get all gung-ho about it, playing the big, tough hero protecting the helpless little woman…

'If you're going to curse me then may I suggest you wait until later?' He stopped so suddenly that Claire cannoned into his back. Muscles rippled as he absorbed the impact and she hastily disentangled herself, not wanting to run the risk of storing away the memory of all that warm, hard flesh.

'All that hissing and spitting under your breath is going to be a real problem when we reach those trees.' He glowered at her. 'I need to be able to hear if there's anyone moving about and your mutterings and mumblings will only hamper things.'

'Oh, well, excuse me! I didn't realise you were such an expert in these matters. Maybe you'd like me to walk downwind so I don't interfere with your olfactory processes?'

'Funny. If you're as good with that gun as you are with your tongue, lady, then we should be safe enough.' He treated her to a smile that was all flashing white teeth and very little warmth. 'However, from the way you're holding it—like a freshly skinned rabbit—I very much doubt it. So no more muttering until we know for certain there are no bogeymen lurking in the woods, eh?'

With that he started walking again, ignoring her as he headed towards the trees. Claire glared after his retreating back before she forced herself to follow him. If they hadn't been in such desperate need of another surgeon at the hospital then she would have left him here and to hell with the consequences. So far as she was concerned, the rebel fighters were welcome to him!

They reached the outer rim of the trees and

stopped. Jude cocked his head to the side, obviously listening for any sound of movement. Claire held her breath because even though the rebels might be welcome to him in theory, she didn't really want him to come to any harm. He glanced at her and there was no trace of laughter on his face this time. He seemed completely focused on the possible dangers and for some reason, she felt almost ridiculously pleased that he was taking her concerns seriously.

'I'm going to skirt round towards the truck through those trees,' he explained in a whisper, pointing out the route he planned to take. 'I want to see if the driver's still in the cab.'

'I'll keep you covered,' she replied equally quietly, quelling a shiver as she looked around. The thought that someone could be hiding in the scrub, watching them, wasn't a pleasant one.

'You do that.' He gave her a quick grin. 'But if you do see anything untoward then make sure it isn't me in your sights, will you? I don't fancy taking a bullet home as a souvenir.'

'I'll do my very best to miss you,' she agreed sweetly, and he laughed.

'Promises, promises—sounds like the story of my life!'

He slipped away before she could say anything, not that she could have come up with anything apposite. Claire sighed because it was the story of *her* life that she could never come up with a witty response when she needed it. She waited in silence, wondering how she would know when he had reached the truck. He was hardly going to holler, *Yoo-hoo, I'm here*, was he?

Was he?

Her heart sank at the thought that he might not be taking this as seriously as she had thought. After all, Dr Slater knew nothing about the dangers of working in this country. Although the majority of the Mwurandans were kindly, God-fearing people, the rebel fighters stopped at nothing to achieve their aims. In the past two months they had stepped up their campaign of terror and everyone working in the country had been warned to be on their guard.

Claire knew that the Worlds Together team would be pulled out if the situation worsened and that she would have to leave with them if that happened. Although she wasn't officially part of their team, she worked alongside them and there would be no excuse for her to stay if they left. Although her visa expired shortly, she wanted to remain here for as long as possible. The thought of going back to England didn't appeal, so she tried not to think about it.

There was still no sign of Jude and she could feel her anxiety rising. Where on earth was he?

All of a sudden she spotted a movement near the rear of the truck and her breath hissed out in relief when she realised it was him. He was crouched down beside the back axle and, as she watched, he began to creep forward, using the truck as a shield as he made his way to the cab. He disappeared from view and she held her breath, praying that nothing had happened to him. If it was a trap, she had let him walk right into it…

He suddenly reappeared and she saw him lift up his hand and beckon to her. He pointed towards the trees, obviously indicating that she should follow the route he had taken. Claire gripped the pistol more firmly as she began to make her way through the undergrowth but her palm was slippery with sweat. Twigs snapped and grasses rustled and her heart pounded harder than ever. She was making so much noise that it would have been far simpler and a whole lot quicker just to run across the clearing. Anyone watching was bound to have heard her!

She reached the truck at last and gasped when she saw that Jude had found Ezra, the driver. He was lying on the ground beside the cab with Jude crouched down beside him. She ran forward and dropped to her knees, staring in horror at the bloody mess that was the man's head.

'Is he dead?'

'No. He's hanging on—just.'

Jude's tone was grim as he elbowed her aside so that he could finish examining the man. Claire didn't protest as this was hardly the time to worry about the social niceties. Long, dexterous fingers tested the man's scalp with a delicacy she had witnessed only a couple of times before in her nursing career. Surprisingly, a lot of surgeons had big, clumsy-looking hands, but Jude's hands were as finely tuned as a pianist's as he felt his way across the driver's skull. He looked up and something warm and sweet rose inside her when she saw the concern in his eyes. Despite appearances to the contrary, Jude Slater possessed more than his share of compassion for his fellow man, it seemed.

'His skull's a mess. There's at least two deep depressions, so heaven only knows the extent of the damage. It looks as though he's been clubbed over the head because he certainly didn't get injuries like these from sitting in that truck, minding his own business.'

'It must have been the rebel fighters,' she said shakily, struggling to get a grip. Thoughts like that certainly weren't ones she wanted to encourage. 'Maybe they thought he was transporting equipment to the airport and that's why they ambushed him. They've been doing a lot of work on the runways recently.'

'You could be right.' He sighed. 'I don't know how we're going to get him to hospital but it certainly won't be on the back of that motorbike of yours. It looks as though I'll have to drive the truck back—if it's still working.'

'I wonder why the rebels didn't take it,' Claire said, frowning. There had been a number of similar incidents recently and on each occasion the vehicle had been stolen.

'Probably because it doesn't work,' Jude suggested with a grimace. 'In which case, we're up the proverbial creek without the proverbial paddle.'

He didn't say anything else as he stood up and climbed into the cab. Claire heard the engine screech as he attempted to start it and her stomach tightened with fear. If there was anyone hiding in the trees then now was the time they would show themselves.

The thought had barely crossed her mind when there was a loud cracking noise and she felt the air shiver as a bullet whistled past her ear. She dropped flat on the ground, her heart pounding as more shots were fired at them. Some hit the truck, others ricocheted off the trees, and all were far too close for comfort.

'Hell's bells! These guys really do mean business, don't they?'

The shock in Jude's voice as he dropped down beside her made her smile despite the precariousness of their position. 'This isn't a theme park experience, Dr Slater. This is the real thing, bullets and all. We really *are* being shot at by the bad guys.'

'That tongue of yours is going to get you into serious trouble one of these days.' He ducked as another volley of shots whined over their heads. Rolling onto his side, he glowered at her. 'OK, Ms Know-it-all, what do you suggest? Do we wave the white flag and appeal to the goodness of their hearts? Or do we try to outmanoeuvre them?'

'I don't think they're very big on the milk of human kindness,' she retorted. 'We have a choice. It's either fight or flight, and I know which I prefer.'

'I'm with you there, although I don't know if this thing is up to it.' He shot a disgusted look at the truck. 'That engine doesn't sound exactly tuned for speed to my ears.'

'Probably not if you're used to something more luxurious but we're not so choosy here,' she snapped, pressing her face into the dirt as more shots whined over their heads. Her voice was muffled as she continued. 'We only have one criterion when it comes to a vehicle: does it work?'

'In that case, we have the prince of trucks at our disposal. It works, although I can't guarantee how fast it goes.' He ducked as another bullet hit the truck then scrambled to his feet. 'I'm going to get the driver into the cab.'

'I'll help you.'

'No, you won't. You stay there and keep your head down. I don't want to have to rescue two casualties, thank you very much.'

Claire fumed as he scuttled on all fours to the cab and wrenched open the door. As the newbie member of the team, he seemed rather too keen to hand out orders. She started to get up then dropped back onto her stomach as another hail of shots pierced the side of the truck just above her head. She could only watch as Jude dragged the driver to the cab and somehow managed to bundle him inside. Sweat was streaming down his face by the time he had finished and there were damp patches on his shirt but he still managed to grin infuriatingly at her.

'So, are you coming, then? Or are you going to stay there and enjoy the scenery?'

Claire gritted her teeth as she belly-crawled to the cab. She wasn't going to fall into the unseemly habit of trading insults with him. Fortunately their attackers didn't appear to know that they had moved because they were still firing at the rear of the truck. It meant they would have surprise on their side when they set off.

Jude gripped her arm as she went to climb into the cab. 'I want you to get into the footwell and stay there. Understand?'

Claire did understand and she wasn't happy about it, either. 'So you can play the all-action hero and get us out of here?'

'Yes.' He grinned at her, a lazy, sexy grin that managed to slip past her defences before she realised it. 'There's no bigger boost to a guy's ego than being able to save a damsel in distress, so don't spoil this for me, sweetheart.'

'I am not and never shall be your sweetheart,' she shot back, hunching down so she could scramble aboard the truck without giving the gunmen an easy target.

'"Never say never" is my motto,' he replied, putting his hand under her backside to give her a boost up.

Claire would have slapped his face if the situation hadn't been so dire. Not just for the cocky remark but for manhandling her as well. She shot into the cab, rolling herself into a ball so she could squeeze into the footwell. The driver was slumped in the passenger seat, mercifully unconscious. That was the one and only good point she could find about the situation, in fact; they wouldn't have to deal with a hysterical patient when they beat a retreat. How they were going to outrun the rebels in this clapped-out old truck was anyone's guess but they didn't have a choice. Handing themselves over to the rebels was a definite non-starter and there was no point trying to fight when…

'I'll take that.' Jude leant down and took the pistol out of her hand. He placed it on the seat then put the truck into gear, swearing colourfully when it failed to engage at the first attempt. There was a hail of shots and the windscreen exploded, showering glass all over the cab, but by that time he had managed to get the truck moving.

They shot out of the trees and careered towards the road as Claire desperately tried to wedge herself into the footwell *and* hold on to the driver to stop him falling off the seat. They hit a rut and she yelped when her head connected painfully with the underside of the dashboard but Jude didn't even spare her a glance. His face was set as he steered the truck across the rutted ground and she shivered. He reminded her of how Andrew had looked that night when he had forced himself on her; he too had been determined to get his own way. It was an effort to push the memory aside as they reached the road and Jude glanced down at her.

'How far is it from here?'

'Five miles, give or take,' she told him, trying to subdue the sickness that had welled up inside her. He *wasn't* Andrew, she reminded herself sharply because she couldn't afford to fall apart.

'Let's hope it's more give than take,' he muttered, jamming his foot down on the accelerator. The rear end of the truck fishtailed before the tyres got a grip and Claire bit her lip. She wasn't going to make a fool of herself by letting him see how scared she was…

'It's going to be OK.' Jude took his hand off the steering wheel and touched her shoulder, and there was a wealth of understanding in his eyes when she looked at him in surprise. He grinned down at her, his handsome face lighting up in a way that made her breath catch but for an entirely different reason this time. 'We're going to make it, Claire. Cross my heart and hope not to die!'

He laughed as he made a cross on his chest

then put his hand back on the steering wheel, but Claire didn't say a word. She didn't dare. If she said anything then she was afraid it would be far too revealing.

Her stomach rolled and she had to force down the wave of panic that rushed up at her. For the past two years, she had felt quite comfortable around the male members of the team. They were simply colleagues and she'd never had a problem working with any of them. However, she knew that state of affairs was about to change. There was just something about Jude Slater that made her feel more aware of him than she'd felt about any man in a very long time. He might not be anything like Andrew but he could prove to be just as dangerous.

Jude could feel the sweat trickling between his shoulder blades. He was scared witless although he had done his best not to let Claire see how he felt. Maybe it was ego which demanded that he mustn't let her know how terrified he was, but he'd be damned if he would start whimpering like a craven coward even though it was what he felt like doing.

He glanced in the wing mirror and felt his stomach try to escape through his boots when he discovered that they were being followed. There were three vehicles behind them and they were gaining on them, too. He jammed his foot down so hard on the accelerator that the engine screeched but he ignored the sound of ancient pistons being put to the ultimate test. If those guys got hold of them then he didn't rate their chances!

'Are they following us?'

He glanced down when she spoke, seeing the fear in her soft grey eyes. He had a better view of her face from this angle and he realised in surprise that she was younger than he had thought, somewhere in her late twenties, perhaps. The cap had been pushed back and he could see strands of honey-gold hair peeking out from under its brim. He'd always had a thing about blondes and he would bet his last pound that she was a natural blonde, too. He would also bet that she had a great figure once she was out of those appalling clothes, although if he didn't keep his mind on the job, he might not get the chance to prove that theory.

'Yep,' he replied laconically, determined not to let her know what he was thinking.

'In that case then can't you make this thing go any faster?' she demanded, glaring up at him.

'If I press down any harder on this pedal, my foot's going to go through the floor,' he retorted, not sure that he appreciated having her demean his efforts to save them. 'It's not my fault if this outfit of yours is too damned mean to buy itself any decent transport, is it?'

'If you mean Worlds Together then it's not my outfit,' she snapped back, bracing herself as they hit another pothole.

Jude grimaced when he heard the crunch of metal because the last thing they needed was a broken axle. He kept his attention on the road although her comment had intrigued him. 'So you don't work for the agency?'

'No. I work with them but not for them.'

He wasn't sure he understood the subtleties of

that distinction but it didn't seem the most pro-
pitious moment to ask her to explain. The rebels
were gaining on them and he grimaced when he
heard shots being fired. 'How much further is it
now?'

'About a mile, maybe less,' she told him, peer-
ing over the edge of the dashboard.

'Get down!' He pushed her head down as a
bullet whined through the cab. He could hear
more shots pinging off the chassis and hunched
over the steering wheel, hoping that none of them
would hit him. He groaned. Yesterday he had
been sitting in an upscale London restaurant, enjoying dinner, and today he was in a beat-up old
truck about to get fried. Talk about the difference a day made!

'Will you *stop* ordering me about! I've been
here a lot longer than you and I know the drill.'

He risked another glance at her when he heard
the anger in her voice and felt his heart give an almighty lurch. Her cap must have been dislodged
when he had shoved her head down and now all
that honey-gold hair was spilling over her shoul-

ders. It was so thick and shiny that he physically ached to run his fingers through it. It was only the thought of them careering off the road if he gave in to the urge that kept his hands on the wheel.

'In that case, what do you suggest?' He raised a mocking black brow, not sure if he appreciated feeling so ridiculously aware of her when the sentiment obviously wasn't reciprocated. 'I could stop the truck and ask them nicely not to shoot at us any more, but somehow I don't think they would be keen to cooperate, do you?'

'Oh, ha-ha, very funny. It must be wonderful to have such a highly developed sense of humour, Dr Slater.'

'I've found it very useful at times,' he replied blandly, then ducked when another volley of shots rained over the cab. The rebels were just yards behind them now and they were gaining fast. He had to do something although his options were seriously limited.

'Here, grab hold of the steering wheel and hold it steady,' he instructed. 'The road's relatively straight from here on, so all you need to do is hang on to it.' He grabbed her hand and clamped it around the base of the steering wheel then picked up the gun.

'But I can't see where we're going!'

'Just hold it steady—that's all you need to do,' Jude said shortly, leaning over so he could see out of the window. He had a clear view of the vehicles that were pursuing them and smiled grimly. Raising the pistol, he took aim and squeezed the trigger—

Nothing happened.

'There aren't any bullets in it.'

It took a whole second for the words to sink in. Jude pulled his head back into the cab and stared, open-mouthed, at the woman in the footwell. 'What did you say?'

'The gun's empty.' She glared up at him, her previously soft grey eyes like shards of flint. 'We're in the business of saving lives, Dr Slater, not taking them. That's why there are no bullets in the gun.'

A dozen different retorts flew into his head and

flew back out again. There was no point asking how or why or even giving vent to his frustration. Jude took the wheel from her and rammed his foot flat on the accelerator, forcing the truck to formerly undiscovered speeds. They rounded a bend and he let out a sigh of relief when he saw the town up ahead. There was an army patrol stationed just outside it and he stamped on the brakes when the soldiers flagged him down. The woman scrambled out of the footwell as the soldiers approached them with their rifles raised.

'We've an injured man on board!' she shouted out of the window. 'We need to get him to hospital.'

The soldiers obviously recognised her because they immediately raised the barrier and waved them through. Jude felt his spirits start to revive a little as he drove along the road. Not only had he managed to outrun the rebel faction, but he would get their patient to hospital as well. Not bad going for his first day in the country, all things considered.

'Take a right at the end of the road and drive

straight across when you reach the crossroads. Sound your horn in case anything's coming but don't stop.'

Jude frowned as he glanced over at her. He would have expected her to be pleased at having got back to the town but she looked almost as edgy now as she had done when they were being pursued.

'You can relax,' he said, injecting an extra-large dollop of honey-coated reassurance into his voice. It was a trick he employed when dealing with particularly nervous patients and it always worked. He was confident that it would work just as well now too. 'We're perfectly safe now.'

'I hate to disillusion you, Dr Slater, but we won't be safe until we're at the hospital.' She smiled thinly as she pointed to a gang of men standing on the corner of the road. 'See those guys over there? They're just waiting for someone like you to come along.'

'Someone like me?' Jude repeated, unconsciously slowing down.

'Keep moving!' She tapped him sharply on the

knee so that his foot hit the accelerator and sent them shooting forward. 'You never, *ever* slow down when you're driving through the town. And it goes without saying that you never stop. Those guys will have this truck off you before you can blink.'

'Oh, come on! You really think I'm just going to hand it over to them?' he scoffed.

'If they hold a gun to your head then yes I do. You'd be a fool not to.' She looked him straight in the eyes and he could tell immediately that she wasn't simply trying to alarm him. 'Vehicles of any description are worth a fortune here. They're far more valuable than a human life and I suggest you remember that.'

She didn't say anything else but she didn't need to; she had said more than enough. Jude's heart plummeted as he drove through the town. He had known it wouldn't be a picnic working here, but he had never imagined it would be *this* bad. By the time he pulled up in front of the hospital, he was beginning to wonder if he should have got onto the plane twelve hours or so ago.

'Stay here while I find a porter,' the woman instructed, jumping down from the cab.

Jude took a deep breath as she disappeared inside, determined to get himself back on even keel. Maybe the situation was far worse than he had expected but he would cope. He had to. Quite apart from the fact that he had been warned at his interview that there was only one flight per month in and out of Mwuranda, he had a lot to prove, didn't he?

When he had left the NHS he had been completely burnt out. The pressure of working the kind of hours he had done, added to the daily struggle to find sufficient qualified staff to allow a scheduled surgery to go ahead, had ground him down. Every time he'd had to explain to a patient that an operation couldn't take place, it had taken its toll on him. It had seemed nothing short of cruel to raise someone's hopes only to dash them.

He'd had such high expectations when he had gone into surgery, too, a genuine desire to help those who had needed it most, but he had become disillusioned. Nevertheless, he would have carried on if it weren't for Maddie, but her death had been the final straw. He had left the NHS and gone into the private sector. It had been either that or give up medicine altogether which he couldn't quite bring himself to do. He had always believed that he had made the right decision, so why did he feel this need to vindicate his actions?

'Right, let's get him out of there.'

Jude swung round when the woman opened the cab door and felt his heart jerk like a puppet having its strings pulled. In that second he realised what was happening and bit back his groan of dismay. It was no longer enough that he proved his worth to his old mentor. Neither was it enough that he proved to himself that he could still hack it. For some inexplicable reason he needed to prove to *her* that he was a damned good surgeon!

CHAPTER THREE

'WE'LL HAVE TO use the triage bay. Resus is full.'

Claire guided the trolley past the queue of people waiting to be seen and elbowed open the door to the triage room. Myrtle, one of the cleaning staff, had just finished mopping the floor and Claire smiled at her. 'Thanks, Myrtle. Can you see if Dr Arnold is anywhere about? We could use his help in here if he's free.'

'I will go and find him for you, Sister.'

Myrtle left the room at her usual sedate pace. None of the local staff ever hurried and they seemed to find it highly amusing when they saw the foreign doctors and nurses rushing around. Claire had found their attitude frustrating when she had first arrived in the country, but she had grown used to it by now. She didn't turn a hair when Benjamin, the porter, took his time positioning the trolley beside the bed although she could tell that Dr Slater was impatient to get on with the job.

'On my count,' she said quietly, determined not to let him know how unsettled she felt by his presence. She grasped hold of a piece of the blanket then checked that he and Benjamin had hold as well. 'One. Two. Three.'

They transferred the injured driver onto the bed and then Bill Arnold arrived.

'You were supposed to be fetching us back a new surgeon not another patient,' he grumbled as he came into the room.

'Stop complaining,' Claire retorted, well used to the middle-aged Yorkshireman's dry sense of humour. 'I could have left the surgeon and just brought you the patient!'

'In other words, count my blessings, eh?' Bill laughed as he came over to the bed and held out his hand. 'Bill Arnold. Nice to have you on board, Dr Slater. What have we got here?'

The two men shook hands before Jude briefly outlined the man's injuries. 'He'll need a CT scan for starters,' he concluded. 'Once I have a better idea what I'm dealing with, I'll want an MRI scan doing as well to check the full extent of soft tissue damage…'

'Whoa! Steady on.'

Bill held up his hand and Jude immediately stopped speaking, although Claire could tell that he wasn't pleased about being interrupted. He was probably more used to people hanging on to his every word, she thought cynically as she began to remove the patient's clothes. Some surgeons seemed to think they ranked second only to God in the pecking order and if that were the case, Jude was in for a nasty shock. The surgeons on the team were treated exactly the same as everyone else, i.e. they were expected to knuckle down and get the job done without a fanfare.

'Is there a problem, Dr Arnold?' Jude asked coolly.

'It's Bill. I dispensed with the formalities a couple of years ago when I retired,' the older man told him. 'And yes, I'm afraid there could be a problem in so far as we don't have access to the equipment you mentioned.'

'What do you mean that you don't have access to it?' Jude demanded. 'Is the radiographer not on duty today?'

'Oh, the radiographer's here all right,' Bill explained easily. 'The problem is the equipment. We don't have a CT scanner or a Magnetic Resonance Imager in the hospital.'

'You don't *have* them,' Jude repeated, looking so stunned by the news that Claire almost felt sorry for him. Obviously it had come as a shock to him to learn that the hospital wasn't equipped with all the usual technology, but had he *really* expected that it would have been? Deliberately, she whipped up her indignation, not wanting to fall into the trap of sympathising with him.

'No. We don't have a CT scanner or access to MRI or PET scanning either, Dr Slater,' she repeated coolly. 'Mwuranda has undergone years of civil unrest and there's no money available for equipment like that. It's difficult enough to maintain an adequate supply of basic drugs, in fact.'

'Then how do you suggest we do our jobs?' he snapped, glaring at her as though he held her personally responsible for the state of the country's medical facilities.

Claire made herself return his stare but the chill in his eyes was unnerving. She couldn't stop her mind darting back to the way Andrew had looked at her whenever she had done something to annoy him. She had to make a determined effort to focus on the present moment. 'The old-fashioned way—through good diagnosis. Isn't that right, Bill?'

'Harrumph, well, yes.' Bill looked uncomfortable about being drawn into the decidedly frosty discussion. He sighed when Jude looked sharply at him. 'I understand your concerns, of course, but in the absence of any modern technology, we just have to do the best we can.'

'I see.' Jude turned and glared at Claire again. 'Well, I want it putting on record that I'm not happy with the situation. Is that clear?'

'As crystal. I shall make a note of your comments in triplicate, Dr Slater, and ensure that the appropriate authorities are informed forthwith.'

Bill looked even more uncomfortable when he heard the sarcasm in Claire's voice but Jude ignored it as he plucked a pair of gloves out of the box. He bent over the patient, his hands moving over the injured man's skull with the same skill and dexterity which Claire had admired earlier. Maybe he was upset about the lack of modern aids, but he was able to contain his emotions while he got on with the job. And it was a salutary reminder of the way her former boyfriend had been able to emotionally detach himself as well.

Claire quickly excused herself and left. She knew it was unprofessional to leave in the middle of an examination but she simply had to get away. Fortunately one of the local nurses was standing in Reception, so Claire asked her if she would assist in triage then made her way to the office to sign in. Every member of staff had to sign in and out whenever they entered or left the building. Although it was a bit of a bind, they all understood how important it was to know where everyone was in case of an emergency. Now Claire sighed as she realised that she hadn't explained the procedure to Dr Slater. It meant that she would have to speak to him again and that was something she had been hoping to avoid. She'd had more than enough of the man for one day!

Lola was sitting behind her desk when Claire opened the office door and she grinned at her. 'I see you made it back safely, then, hon.'

'Only just.' Claire scrawled her name on the sheet then poured herself a cup of coffee. Walking over to the one and only easy chair, she flopped down onto its lumpy cushions. 'We found the truck on our way back. And the driver.'

'And?' Lola prompted when she paused to sip some of the muddy brown brew that passed for coffee.

'*And* we ended up starring in our very own version of the shoot-out at the OK Corral.' She grimaced as she put the cup on a pile of medical journals which served as a coffee table in the absence of anything else. 'That coffee is disgusting! How long has it been stewing in the pot?'

'Who knows?' Lola dismissed the coffee's pedigree with a wave of her hand. Anxiety was etched all over her face as she looked at Claire in concern. 'Are you sure you're all right? It must have been real scary for you, so don't think you have to pull that stiff-upper-lip routine you Brits are famous for. If you want to bawl your eyes out then go right ahead.'

'I'm fine. Really,' Claire assured her. 'OK, so it was a bit hairy at the time, but I was too angry to be really scared.'

'Angry?' Lola repeated. 'You mean with the guys who were shooting at you?'

'No. With Dr Jude Tobias Slater!'

Claire stood up and started to pace the room, her temper rocketing as she thought about all the things he had done that day. Ignoring her instructions to stay with the motorbike had been his first offence and his second had been the high-handed way he had taken charge. Maybe they were only minor misdemeanours in most people's eyes but

they were far more than that to her. Jude Slater
had tried his best to undermine her at every turn
and she had too much experience of the harm it
could cause to allow that to happen to her again.

She turned and glowered at Lola. 'The guy is a
liability! He's pushy and overbearing and, what's
more, he seems to think that he knows everything
about what it takes to survive out here when he
knows nothing at all. Would you believe that he
actually expected there would be an MRI scanner in the hospital?'

'It's his first mission, though, hon.'

Lola shrugged, obviously trying to defuse the
situation, but Claire didn't want it to be defused.
She wanted there to be tension between her and
Jude, and lots of it, too, because it would help
to blot out everything else. The one thing she
mustn't allow herself to do was to like him.

'So?' she scoffed. 'I remember when you arrived, Lola. It was your first mission as well, but
you didn't expect there to be all kinds of fancy
equipment here, did you?'

'Ah, but I came straight from an inner-city public hospital, so my expectations were already fairly low.'

'I suppose so.' Claire gave a grudging smile. 'From what you've told me, conditions there weren't all that much better than they are here.'

'You got that right, hon.'

Lola laughed. However, Claire knew that her friend was wondering why she had taken such an obvious dislike to the newest member of their team. There was no way she could explain that Jude reminded her of Andrew, not when she had told nobody about her former partner, so she remained silent and, after a moment, Lola carried on.

'Dr Slater doesn't have my kind of background, Claire. I checked his file while you were out and discovered that he's been working in some fancy private hospital in London for the past five years. How's he going to have any experience of real life when he's been mixing with rich folks like that?'

'In other words, I should cut him some slack— is that what you're saying?'

'I guess so. OK, so maybe you two didn't hit it off, but don't let first impressions colour your judgement. You guys are going to have to work together and it's going to make life extremely difficult if you're at each other's throats all the time.'

Claire knew that Lola was right. However, the thought of having to work with him was too disturbing to deal with right then. She bolted down the rest of her coffee, fixing a smile into place when Lola looked at her in concern.

'Don't worry. I'm not about to do anything rash. I forgot to tell Dr Slater that he needs to sign in, so I'd better go and do it before I forget.'

'You do that, hon. And I bet you find that he isn't nearly as bad as you thought he was.'

Claire didn't say anything. It would serve no purpose to argue with Lola. However, as she left the office, she knew that the one thing she wouldn't do was try to improve her opinion of Jude Slater. She intended to keep him at arm's length and the more things she could find to dislike about him, the easier it would be.

* * *

'I'll remove this section of bone. Then we can see how extensive the bleeding is.'

Jude bent over the operating table as he carefully eased the shattered section of bone from the man's skull. It was delicate work and even the tiniest slip could have the most horrendous consequences for the patient but he knew that he possessed the necessary skills. He was a first-rate surgeon despite the fact that he spent most of his time these days stripping out varicose veins.

The thought that he wasn't utilising his talent as he should be doing was unsettling. He had always believed that opting for the private sector had been the right decision. The perks which came with the job were all too obvious: an excellent salary; working hours which allowed him a healthy social life; an environment in which to work where the very best facilities were always available. However, he had to admit that he had become increasingly bored of late. Most of the work he did was purely routine and there was very little that stretched him. An operation like this was completely different. One slip and the patient could be left severely incapacitated and the thought put him on his mettle. As he suctioned away the massive haematoma that had formed inside the man's skull, Jude realised in surprise that he was *enjoying* himself.

'Clamp.' He rapped out the instruction, nodding when the nurse at his side slapped the instrument into his palm. He clamped the damaged blood vessel then carefully removed two minute splinters of bone. Fortunately the meninges—the protective membranes which covered the brain—hadn't been pierced, so once he had cauterised the vein, the bleeding stopped. Nevertheless, it was another hour before he was satisfied that he had done all he could. It was out of his hands now and up to nature to run its course.

Jude glanced at Bill Arnold, who was acting as his anaesthetist. 'I'm going to call it a day. There's not much more I can do for him.'

'From what I saw, you did more than most would have attempted,' Bill replied as he began to reverse the anaesthetic. 'Good work, son.'

Normally, Jude would have bridled if anyone had called him *son* but for some reason he was touched by the compliment. 'Thanks,' he said lightly, not wanting the older man to guess that it meant anything to him.

He left Theatre, dropping his disposable cap into the bin on his way out before making his way to the changing room only to stop short when he opened the door and found Claire sitting on one of the benches. She immediately sprang to her feet when she saw him and he couldn't help noticing how defensive she looked.

'I forgot to tell you about signing in,' she said quickly, and he winced when he heard the hostility in her voice.

It had been obvious when they were in Triage that he wasn't exactly flavour of the month and he could only conclude that it was because of what had happened earlier in the day. Maybe he should have deferred to her instead of taking over like that, but in his own defence, he had been more concerned about their safety than her injured feelings. He had been right, too, he assured himself, so he would be damned if he would apologise when he had got them safely back to the hospital.

'So tell me now,' he said flatly, stripping off the top of his scrub suit and tossing it into the dirty-linen hamper. There was a stack of clean towels on a shelf, so he picked one up and flung it over his shoulder then glanced round when she didn't reply. 'Look, I don't want to rush you but I would like to take a shower this side of Christmas, if it's all right with you.'

'Yes, of course. Sorry.' A rush of colour swept up her face as she hurried on. 'You need to sign in every time you come into work and sign out again each time you leave. The sheets are kept in the office, so if you could sign out after you finish up here that would be great.'

'And what do I do after that?' He shrugged when she looked blankly at him. 'Am I supposed to stay in the hospital, or what? I've no idea about our living arrangements.'

'Oh, I see. I should have explained it all to you before, but things got a bit hectic after we found the truck—' She broke off, obviously reluctant to talk about what had gone on earlier.

Jude sighed as he realised that his assessment had been spot on. She *did* harbour a grudge about the way he had railroaded her and it was going to make life extremely stressful in the coming weeks if she didn't get over it. He was just debating whether he should rustle up some sort of apology when she continued.

'The Worlds Together team doesn't actually live in the hospital. They use the old college as their base, so you'll be staying there.'

'I see. And how do I get there? Do I walk, in which case I'll need directions. Or is there transport available?' he asked, deciding there was no point worrying about what might happen. He would just have to take each day as it came and hope that she would do the same.

'You'll be ferried to and from the hospital in one of the trucks. It not only saves time but it's safer.' She glanced at her watch and frowned. 'In fact, the day shift should be leaving in about ten minutes' time, so you can catch a lift back to the college with them.'

'It doesn't sound as though it's going to be a whole lot of fun working here if we have to sign in and out, *and* use only the official form of transport,' Jude observed dryly. 'The last time I had restrictions like these imposed on me, I was at boarding school.'

'We aren't here to have fun, Dr Slater. We're here to help the people of this country. It certainly won't help them if you get yourself killed.'

'It wouldn't be too great from my point of view, either,' Jude retorted. She had the knack of making him feel as though he was lacking in some way and it wasn't a feeling he enjoyed. 'Anyway, I'd better take that shower,' he said, swinging round. 'I'd hate to blot my copybook again by keeping everyone waiting.'

'You'll be picked up outside the main doors. I'll let the driver know you're coming,' she said shortly, ignoring his final comment.

Jude sighed as she left, aware that it had been extremely childish to say that. There was no point antagonising her when they were going to have to work together. It was just that he wasn't used to people taking such an obvious dislike to him and definitely not a woman. Despite the fact that he made no bones about the fact that he wasn't interested in commitment, most women seemed to enjoy his company and were eager to spend time with him, but not this woman. He'd got the distinct impression that she had only come to find him out of a sense of duty and the thought rankled. He turned on the water, wondering why he was so bothered about her opinion. It shouldn't have mattered a jot what she thought of him but it did. He wanted her to like him—how pathetic was that?

Jude finished showering and dressed then made his way to the front entrance. There was a group of people sitting on the steps, obviously waiting to be collected, so he went and joined them. One of the women grinned at him as he sat down.

'So you're the new guy, are you? I heard that Claire was going to the airport this afternoon to collect you.'

'Jude Slater at your service.' He smiled as he held out his hand. 'And you are?'

'Lesley Morris. One of the nurses,' the woman explained as they shook hands.

'Nice to meet you, Lesley. So far I've met Bill Arnold and a couple of the local staff but that's basically it. How many of us are there on the team?'

'Nine at the moment, although it can and does fluctuate. There are five nurses and four doctors now that you've arrived.' Lesley pointed to a group of women in front of them. 'That's Kelly, Amy and Sasha—they're all nurses. Lola, who's our administrator, is also a nurse and helps out whenever necessary. Javid and Matt are the other two doctors on the team. Matt's working tonight, so you'll meet him at dinner before he goes on duty. And Javid should be along any second now.'

'What about Claire?' Jude frowned as he looked at the women. 'You said there were five nurses, so where does Claire fit in?'

'Oh, she's not part of our team,' Lesley explained. 'Although I don't know how we'd manage without her. If you need something doing around here then Claire's the woman to ask. We call her our very own miracle worker!'

'Praise indeed,' he replied lightly, wondering who Claire worked for if she wasn't part of the Worlds Together team. Although his knowledge of the agency's set-up was pretty sketchy, he didn't recall anyone mentioning at his interview that they would be working with another aid agency, yet who else could she be working for? He was just about to ask Lesley when the truck arrived and everyone stood up.

Jude followed them down the steps and waited his turn to board. Lesley had moved to the front. She patted the seat, indicating that he should sit next to her, so he climbed over everyone's legs and squeezed into the gap. The driver was just about to fasten the tailgate when Jude saw Claire coming out of the hospital and he felt his heart give an almighty lurch. She had shed the ugly old boiler suit and was wearing a light grey dress with a prim little white collar and cuffs. She had also got rid of the baseball cap and her blonde hair was caught back at the nape of her neck.

Jude's pulse began to drum as he took stock of the gently rounded curves of her breasts and hips, the purity of her profile. There was no doubt that she was a very beautiful and desirable woman and he would have needed to be dead from the neck up *and* down not to notice that fact…

'Do you want a lift, Sister? I can call at the convent on my way back if it will save you having to wait.'

Jude heard what the driver said but it was a full minute before the words registered and he gasped. It felt as though everything was happening in slow motion as he watched Claire walk over to the truck and climb on board. She was obviously popular because everyone greeted her with a smile although he didn't. He couldn't. He could neither smile nor speak as he watched her take her place on the bench. He closed his eyes, wondering if his mind was playing tricks. It had been a stressful day and it was understandable if he was a little…well, confused.

The truck set off with a lurch and Jude opened his eyes, expecting that the scene would have changed. It hadn't. Claire was sitting serenely on the bench, her hands lightly clasped in her lap. A breeze suddenly blew into the truck and he saw her lift up her hand to tuck a loose strand of hair behind her ear. Jude felt a huge great wave of regret wash over him. Even though he knew he had no business feeling that way, he couldn't help it. It just seemed like such a terrible waste. Claire might be beautiful and desirable but she was also strictly off limits to him or to any other man.

The fact was that *Sister* Claire was a nun!

CHAPTER FOUR

CLAIRE COULD FEEL Jude Slater staring at her although she didn't look at him. Seeing him standing in the changing room had awoken feelings that she had never imagined she would experience again. She had honestly thought that she was incapable of feeling desire after what Andrew had done, but there was no point pretending. The sight of Jude's leanly muscular body had unlocked a whole host of emotions and now she just wanted to forget about them.

When Javid Khan asked her what had happened on the way back from the airfield, she sighed under her breath. She would have preferred not to talk about what had gone on but she could hardly say so in case it started people speculating. The last thing she wanted was everyone thinking that she had a problem with Dr Slater even if it were true.

'It was a bit of a rough ride,' she said lightly, trying to avoid going into detail. 'Basically, the rebel fighters had set up a trap and we walked straight into it. We were lucky to get back here.'

'That's an understatement if ever I heard one.' Javid grinned at her. 'I saw the state of that truck. There were so many bullet holes in it that you could have used it as a colander!'

Everyone laughed, although Claire noticed that Jude didn't join in. She shook her head when Kelly asked her how the driver was doing. 'I wasn't there during surgery, so you'll have to ask Dr Slater.'

Kelly repeated the question to Jude and Claire felt her heart skip a beat when she heard the edge in his voice as he explained that although the driver had come through the operation, the next twenty-four hours were critical. She shot him a wary glance but for some reason he seemed reluctant to look at her. Claire frowned as she studied the rigid set of his jaw. He hadn't looked this uptight when they had been fleeing from their attackers, so what was wrong with him?

The question nagged away at her for the rest of the journey. When the driver pulled up in front of the college, Claire realised that she wouldn't be able to rest until she found out the answer. Maybe it had nothing to do with her but the least she could do was to ascertain if Jude had some sort of a problem. After all, she was supposed to be helping him settle in and, so far, she had done very little towards that goal.

She told the driver that she had decided to spend the night at the college and followed the others out of the truck. She had stayed there many times before, mainly when there had been a problem getting back to the convent. There was no real reason why she should continue living there, in fact. Her role as an observer for the WHO had long since ended but it had seemed easier to stick to the arrangements. She knew that the nuns had come to rely on her. Most of them were elderly and she helped out as much as she could with the children they cared for. What would happen when she left Mwuranda was open to question but she knew that the nuns wouldn't be able to continue running the orphanage if they didn't get extra help.

'Oh, great! You've decided to stay over, have you?' Lesley looped her arm through Claire's as they walked into the building together.

'I thought it'd be easier than asking the driver to take me all the way back to the convent,' she explained, skirting around the real reason for her change of plans. She glanced round when Jude and Sasha followed them inside and couldn't help noticing that once again he avoided looking in her direction.

'I don't know why you don't move in with us,' Lesley declared. 'Oh, I know you like to help the sisters, but they're going to have to do without you at some point, Claire. You're due to return to England soon, aren't you?'

'I suppose so.'

'Don't you want to go home?' Lesley demanded, frowning. 'I'd have thought you would have had more than enough of this place by now. How long is it since you first came out here?'

'Almost two years.' Claire replied distractedly as she watched Jude drop his bag by the door then wander into the communal sitting room. If she was to find out what was troubling him then it would be best to get it over sooner rather than later, she decided. If he did have a problem then she knew from experience how quickly it could affect the smooth running of the team and that was something she wanted to avoid. They were under so much pressure as it was that even the smallest problem could rapidly turn into a major issue.

She turned and smiled at Lesley. 'I just need a word with Dr Slater—make sure he's up to speed about what's expected of him. I didn't get chance to run through all the dos and don'ts with him before.'

'No wonder. You were too busy dodging bullets from the sound of it,' Lesley retorted.

Claire laughed. 'Something like that. Anyway, is it OK if I use the spare bed in your room?'

'Be my guest. Another pair of hands to swat the bugs is always welcome!'

Lesley sketched her a wave and headed up the stairs. The rest of the team had already disappeared and Claire guessed that they would be using the time to shower before dinner. It was the ideal opportunity to speak to Jude on his own.

She went into the sitting room, feeling her pulse leap when she found him standing by the window. He had his back towards her and there was an air of dejection about the way he stood there, staring out across the grounds. Had he suddenly realised what he had let himself in for? she wondered. From what Lola had told her, this type of work was a million miles away from what he was used to and she couldn't help wondering what had prompted him to apply for the job in the first place. Had it been just a desire to help his fellow man? Or had there been another reason?

He suddenly turned and Claire hurriedly squashed the thought when she saw him stiffen as he caught sight of her. He seemed less than entranced to see her and she found herself wishing that she hadn't bothered seeking him out. So what if he had a problem: why should she care? However, deep down she knew that she owed it to the team to find out what was troubling him.

'I just wanted to check that you're all right.' She shrugged. 'I didn't get chance to discuss any issues you may have earlier, I'm afraid. There was too much going on.'

'Don't worry about me. I'm fine.' He moved away from the window and she could see a nerve beating in his jaw as he crossed the room.

'Oh, right, well, good. I know it must seem a bit restricting to have to stick to all these rules and regulations, but we have to be careful.'

'Of course. And I'm sure I'll get used to it.' He stopped, one dark brow arching when she failed to move out of his way. 'Was there anything else you wanted to say to me?'

'Er…no, not at all.'

Claire hurriedly stepped aside to let him pass, wondering why she had the feeling that he was upset about *her*. She gave herself a mental shake because now she was being ridiculous. He was probably tired and stressed after everything that had happened that day and the best thing she could do was to give him some space. A lot of new recruits found it overwhelming to be thrown in at the deep end, and Jude Slater had been thrown into deeper water than most. The fact that he had coped so well was to his credit.

The thought was more than a little alarming in view of the fact that she was determined not to find anything good about him. Claire hurried from the room and headed upstairs. Lesley was in the bathroom when she got to their room, so she sat down on the spare bed and waited for her to finish. She didn't have a change of clothes with her but she knew that her friend would lend her something to wear.

She sighed as she pulled the clip out of her hair and shook it free. She couldn't remember the last time she'd had anything decent of her own to wear. Normally she wore scrubs in work and either overalls or one of the nuns' dresses after she finished her shift. It was safer not to draw attention to herself when she was travelling to and from the hospital and the plain grey dresses the nuns wore allowed her a certain anonymity. However, all of a sudden she found herself wishing that she had something pretty to wear that night, something that would make her feel like a woman. And it was such a shock to want to proclaim her femininity that she felt fear sweep through her. She had honestly thought that she would never feel this way again, so what had changed? Was it the fact that the scars had started to heal and she was feeling more confident, or was there another reason?

Unbidden a face sprang to her mind and her heart began to pound when she recognised Jude Slater's handsome features. Did she want to look pretty and feminine for *his* sake? Hadn't she learned her lesson, learned how foolish it was to allow a man that much power over her? Obviously not. However, there was no way that she was going down that road again. No way at all!

* * *

Jude collected his bag from the porch and made his way upstairs, pausing when he came to the first-floor landing. Sasha had told him that he could choose whichever bedroom he fancied but he didn't want to invade anyone else's territory. He had made enough gaffes for one day.

Jude's mouth thinned at the thought as he made his way along the landing. The doors to most of the rooms were standing open and it was obvious from the clutter lying around that they were in use. He came to a room halfway along the landing and glanced inside, pausing when he spotted Claire sitting on one of the beds. She had removed the clip and her blonde hair cascaded over her shoulders like a silken waterfall. Jude's palms began to tingle as he stared at the shimmering mass of gold. How he ached to touch her hair, to bury his face in it and savour its softness…

He forced himself to move on, feeling like the lowest kind of lowlife. She was a nun, for heaven's sake! A woman who had taken a vow of chastity. Thoughts like that were totally abhorrent and needed to be nipped in the bud yet it was far more difficult than it should have been. Crazy though he knew it was, he couldn't help wondering if she might be persuaded to change her mind about her chosen vocation...

'Idiot!' Jude didn't realise he had spoken out loud until a head poked round a door further along the corridor.

'Far be it from me to disagree with you, but that seems a tad harsh. Who or what is the idiot in question?'

'Me.' A couple of strides took Jude to the room and to the owner of the head who turned out to be a man roughly his age with dark red hair and what looked like a million freckles on his face. Jude held out his hand and grinned ruefully. 'I'm the idiot. I'm also Jude Slater, the new recruit. How do you do?'

'Nice to meet you, Jude.' The man uncoiled himself and straightened up, towering over Jude's not inconsiderable six-foot frame. 'Matt Kearney at your service. As well as being one of the doctors, I'm the general dogsbody around here—I do a bit of this and a bit of that, plus a lot of the other. If there's anything you need then I can usually get it for you. Within reason, of course.'

'That's good to know.' Jude laughed, taking an immediate liking to the other man. He glanced into the room, taking note of the colourful rugs on the bare floorboards and the bright cotton throw on the bed, and nodded. 'Hmm, not an idle boast from the look of it. You've made it very cosy in there, I must say.'

'It all helps, doesn't it?' Matt looked around with an air of satisfaction. 'Everything is locally made, so it's a win-win situation. I get to enjoy some home comforts while I'm here and at the same time help to boost the local economy. The best thing we can do to help the people in this country, apart from patching them up, of course, is to provide them with a living. That's why I'm hoping to get one of the big designer stores on board when I get back to Blighty. I mean, the Chelsea set would go a bomb for stuff like this, wouldn't they?'

'They would indeed,' Jude agreed, thinking how very true that was. Indigenous arts and crafts were very much of the moment with those who had the wherewithal to pay for them. Why, he himself had spent a small fortune on some rugs very similar to the ones on Matt's floor. He had never given any thought to who had produced them, just liked them and handed over the money for them. How much of it had gone to the people who had made them? he found himself wondering. Probably very little, he decided, and the thought made him feel uncomfortable. Maybe he needed to think more about the ethics of what he bought in future.

'Right. I'd better go and find myself a room. Is there one free on this floor or should I try the floor above?' Jude said briskly because he was becoming heartily sick of all these reminders as to his shortcomings.

'Oh, stick to this floor unless you're a fan of bats and don't mind sharing with them.' Matt grinned. 'They're not bad roommates, especially when you're on nights as they prefer to sleep through the day. However, their personal hygiene does leave a lot to be desired.' He pointed along the corridor. 'The end room is free, so help yourself. The women prefer to bunk up together, but we guys don't go in for communal living in quite the same way. Dinner's at seven but don't bother with the black tie. We're very informal. So long as you're wearing clothes, you'll do.'

Matt went back into his room, leaving Jude to get settled in. He unpacked his bag and laid out his shaving gear on the old marble-topped washstand. He hadn't noticed a bathroom on his travels but he would track it down at some point. Glancing at his watch, he kicked off his shoes and lay down on the bed as exhaustion caught up with him. He had been on the go for the past twenty-four hours and a nap would help to recharge his batteries. He was certainly going to need them charging too. From what he had seen so far, this definitely wasn't going to be a walk in the park. No, he would be kept busy from dawn to dusk which wasn't a bad thing if it stopped him thinking thoughts he had no right to harbour.

Closing his eyes, Jude let his mind drift, his heart sinking when it immediately sailed off towards the one direction it was banned from taking. Claire was off limits! If he repeated it often enough then surely it would sink in?

CHAPTER FIVE

DINNER THAT NIGHT was a lively affair. Whether it was the fact that they had someone new in the form of Jude Slater to entertain them, but everyone seemed in very high spirits. Claire collected her plate from Moses, their cook, and carried it to the table. They always ate together of an evening, gathered at one end of the huge refectory table that ran the full length of the dining room. Lesley had lit the storm lantern and she placed it on the table. She grinned when Jude looked at it in surprise as he came back from the serving hatch.

'It's less for atmosphere than practicality,' Lesley informed him. 'It's rare we ever get through an evening meal without the power going off, so we follow the old Girl Guide motto and make sure we're prepared.'

'Oh, I see.' Jude glanced round but there was only one seat left, the one next to Claire. His reluctance to sit in it was obvious and it stung. For some reason she had become persona non grata in his eyes.

Claire edged her chair away as he sat down, not wanting to risk coming into contact with him. Lesley had lent her a dress, quite a pretty one too, made from pale pink cotton with short sleeves and a modestly scooped neck. She hadn't bothered fastening back her hair, just left it loose around her shoulders, and she was aware of Jude's eyes skimming over her but determinedly applied herself to her meal. What he thought of her appearance was neither here nor there!

'This is rather good. What is it exactly?'

She glanced round when he spoke, feeling her heart catch when she found herself staring straight into his eyes. A rich warm hazel with flecks of gold around the irises, they seemed to draw her in and hold her spellbound. It was only when she saw one elegant black brow arch that she remembered he was waiting for her to answer.

'Mutton stew. It's one of Moses' signature dishes, so he tends to make it quite often,' she gabbled. She forked up a mouthful of the spicy concoction to give herself time to calm down but her heart was still behaving in a highly erratic fashion. 'Apparently, his mother used to make it for him—it's her recipe.'

'Clever mum. And clever Moses for getting the recipe off her.' Jude forked up some of the vegetable that had been served with it and grimaced. 'I'm not sure about this though. It's a bit like sweet potato but incredibly dry and stringy.'

'It's yam. I wasn't too keen on it either but I've got used to it now. The trick is to never eat it on its own. Mix some gravy into it to make it more palatable,' she advised, feeling a little easier now that the conversation was centred on such mundane matters.

'Mmm, better, although I doubt if I'll be adding it to my shopping list when I get home.'

Javid claimed his attention then and he turned away. Claire continued to eat, letting the conversation flow over her. Normally, she would have joined in but for some reason she felt strangely detached that night. When the lights suddenly went out, plunging the room into darkness apart from the glow from the hurricane lamp, it was a relief. There was less chance of anyone noticing how quiet she was now and remarking on it.

They rounded off the meal with fresh fruit and coffee, although Claire passed on the coffee. Experience had taught her that it was better to avoid the malodorous brew that Moses concocted with such delight.

'My heaven!' Jude put down his cup and shook his head. 'That stuff is lethal. I mean, I like strong coffee but that's in a league of its own!'

Everyone laughed and started to regale him with tales of their own experiences with Moses' pièce de résistance although Claire didn't join in. All of a sudden everything that had transpired that day seemed to have caught up with her. She felt a shudder run through her and then another...

'Are you all right?'

A lean, tanned hand closed around hers and her heart seemed to stop. Now it wasn't just the fear she had felt when they had outrun the rebel fighters that was causing her such distress but other memories, far more terrifying: Andrew holding her hands as he forced her down onto the bed; trapping her there with his weight as he ignored her pleas to stop…

A moan escaped her lips, like the tiny cry of an animal in pain, and she felt Jude's fingers tighten. 'If you're going to faint then mind the table. You don't need a lump on your head to add to your woes.'

It was so ridiculous that Claire laughed. She laughed and she laughed until she couldn't stop. Everyone had stopped talking and they were staring at her but all she could do was laugh. Jude was worrying about her getting a bump on her head while she was remembering being raped!

'That's enough now, Claire. You need to stop.' Jude felt a wave of alarm engulf him as he gathered Claire into his arms. She was trembling uncontrollably and his hold on her tightened a fraction more. What had caused her to behave this way was a mystery; however, he was less concerned about why it had happened than how he could stop it. She was going to make herself ill if she carried on like this.

'Come on, Claire. Take a nice deep breath.' Holding her at arm's length, he looked into her eyes, feeling more concerned than ever when she stared blankly back at him.

'What's wrong with her?' Lesley came over and crouched down beside them, her pleasant face filled with concern.

'I've no idea but she'd be better off upstairs.'

Jude stood up and helped Claire out of her seat, swinging her up into his arms when her legs buckled. There was silence in the dining room as he carried her into the hall and up the stairs. Obviously what had happened had come as a shock to everyone.

'Here, put her down on the bed.' Lesley had followed them upstairs. Scooping up the dress Claire had worn earlier, she unceremoniously tossed it onto the floor. 'You don't need to stay, Jude. I'll look after her.'

Jude reluctantly laid Claire down on the bed,

unable to understand why he was so loath to surrender her to Lesley's care. He had vowed after he had left the NHS that never again would he allow himself to become emotionally involved and he had applied that doctrine to every aspect of his life, too, not just to the patients he treated but the women he dated as well. Oh, he did everything that was expected of him and more, but he always held part of himself in reserve. It was a system that had worked well, one that he'd had no intention of changing, and yet all of a sudden all his protective urges were rushing to the fore. Relinquishing Claire to someone else's care was the last thing he could do, not even if his life had depended on it!

'Has anything like this ever happened before?' he said roughly, ignoring Lesley's offer as it was easier than explaining his need to stay. Admitting that he could no more abandon Claire than he could fly to the moon was the last thing he intended to do.

'No. Never. Claire is normally so calm and controlled. Nothing ever seems to faze her.' Lesley shook her head. 'I really don't understand what's happened tonight.'

'Could it be the stress of the attack?' he suggested, reaching out to smooth back a strand of silky blonde hair before he realised what he was doing. His hand fell to the pillow as a feeling of despondency engulfed him. He had no right to touch her, no right at all. 'It was pretty tense,' he continued thickly. 'I have to confess that I didn't think we were going to make it at one point.'

'It's possible, I suppose, although it isn't the first time that she's been involved in an incident like that. A couple of times the truck ferrying her to the convent has come under attack.' Lesley sighed. 'Maybe it's been building up for a while. I mean, she's been out here for two years now and that's a long time to be under such constant pressure. What happened today could have been the final straw.'

'It sounds likely,' Jude agreed, darkly. Maybe it was expected of the nuns but to his mind there was only so much any human being could take. And Claire had obviously reached her limit.

He stood up abruptly, knowing that now wasn't the time to kick up a fuss. It didn't mean that he intended to let the matter drop; however, he would wait until he could speak to whoever was in charge of the convent before he made his views clear. Once again the realisation that he was allowing his emotions to get the better of him was very hard to swallow and he turned away. 'I've some sleeping pills in my room. I'll go and fetch them. The best thing for her now is a good night's sleep—'

'I don't want any pills. I don't need them.'

Jude glanced round when Claire spoke, relieved to see that she seemed far more alert. Although she was extremely pale still, her eyes were focused when they met his. 'I apologise for making a scene,' she continued huskily. 'It won't happen again, I assure you.'

She went to get up but Jude stopped her. As his hand closed around her wrist, he found himself marvelling at how slender it was. He could, quite literally, encircle it with his little finger and thumb. Once again all his protective urges rushed to the fore and once again he felt shock hit him in the gut.

He didn't do this! He didn't allow himself to feel this strongly any more. If he hadn't cared so much then it would never have hit him so hard when Maddie had died. He had learned a valuable lesson then, learned how to detach himself and feel only on the surface, never deep down; yet it was different where Claire was concerned. He couldn't seem to take that essential step back. What was going on here? Why had he, Mr Deliberately Indifferent, suddenly turned into Mr Overly Protective?

Jude had no idea what the answer was but it scared him to know that he had undergone such a massive change in such a short space of time. He had been in Mwuranda for less than a day and already he was turning into a whole different person, so help him!

Claire could feel the coolness of Jude's fingers on her hot flesh and shivered. Now that the memory of that dreadful night had started to fade, she felt better able to cope, although how she was going to explain her behaviour was another matter. Maybe it would be safer to settle for Lesley's explanation, that she had been under pressure for so long and tonight it had caught up with her. Telling everyone what Andrew had done was out of the question. She only had to recall what he had said when she had warned him that she would go to the police in an attempt to stop him. He had laughed in her face as he had stated that it would be her word against his, and who was going to believe the word of an embittered woman who had been dumped by her boyfriend?

'You need to rest even if you won't take a sleeping pill.'

Jude's voice cut through her thoughts and she shuddered. She mustn't think about the past. She must focus on the present and that meant making sure nobody found out what had happened to her. Even if everyone believed her, did she really want to become an object of pity in their eyes? Someone who needed to be treated differently? A victim? Was that how she wanted *Jude* to view her?

The thought was more than she could bear for some reason. It was an effort to concentrate as he continued. 'I suggest you take a few days off and give yourself a breathing space. If you want me to have a word with whoever's in charge then I'm more than happy to do so.'

'That won't be necessary,' Claire said quickly. 'And as for taking time off, well, I'm afraid that's out of the question. We're working at full stretch as it is and if I take time off then it will put the rest of the team under even more pressure.' Easing her wrist out of his grasp, she stood up before he could stop her. 'I'm fine, Dr Slater. There's no need to worry about me.'

'I disagree. It's obvious that you're far from fine.' There was an edge to his voice now but why should he feel angry about her desire to forget what had happened tonight? Why should he care? Before Claire could work it out he continued in the same biting tone.

'I appreciate that you consider your work a vocation rather than a job but it would be foolish to risk your health. I shall speak to the Mother Superior and explain that you need to rest, Sister.'

Sister? Claire wasn't sure why Jude had called her that until she saw the dawning comprehension on Lesley's face. She bit back a gasp. He thought she was a nun! Oh, she could understand how he had reached that conclusion. Between her choice of clothes and the fact that she lived at the convent, it was an easy mistake to have made. She was about to set him straight when it struck her that it might be better if she allowed him to carry on believing it.

Even though she hated to admit it, Jude Slater *disturbed* her. He made her think about things she hadn't thought about in a long time, made her aware of her own femininity in a way she didn't welcome, and it scared her. She had thought that part of her life was over, that never again would she be attracted to a man. Although she worked with the male members of the team on a daily basis, she had never had a problem with any of them—they were colleagues, no more than that.

However, Jude was different. *She* felt differently around him. More vulnerable. More aware. Maybe it would be better if he continued to think that she was off limits.

'Oh, but Claire isn't—' Lesley began, but Claire cut her off.

'I shall speak to Sister Julie myself,' she said firmly, shooting a warning glance at her friend. 'There's no need for you to become involved, Dr Slater.'

'Fine. It's your decision, Sister.' He nodded dismissively, his face devoid of expression. 'Just make sure you get some rest. You obviously need it.'

He didn't say anything more before he left. Claire listened to the sound of his footsteps echoing along the corridor, followed by a door closing, and only then let out the breath she hadn't even known she was holding. There was definitely something about Jude Slater that set all her internal alarm bells ringing...

'OK, so what exactly is going on?' Lesley placed her hands on her hips and fixed Claire with a hard stare. 'Why did you allow the gorgeous, *sexy* Dr Slater to think you're a nun?'

'Because he is gorgeous. And sexy. And because I don't want him practising his gorgeously sexy charms on me.'

'Why ever not!' Lesley exclaimed. 'Oh, I know we're not supposed to form relationships but that's never stopped anyone, has it? I mean, look at Sasha and Javid. They're totally smitten but it hasn't affected their work. So what's to stop you and the gorgeous Jude indulging in an *affaire de coeur*? You're both young, free and single, plus it's obvious that he's interested...'

'Of course he isn't interested!' Claire denied hotly. Colour ran up her face when Lesley treated her to an old-fashioned look. 'He isn't. He's just one of those men who can't stop themselves hitting on a woman. That's all it is.'

'If you say so,' Lesley replied, making it clear that she didn't believe her. Reaching under her pillow, she pulled out her pyjamas. 'Right, time for beddy-byes, I think. There's clean jammies in the top drawer of the chest, so help yourself.'

She headed off to the bathroom, leaving Claire to sort out her night attire. Opening the drawer, she took out the first set of pyjamas she came to. They were made from plain white cotton, very prim and virginal, perfectly in keeping with her new persona, in fact. She smiled wryly as she undressed and slipped them on. *Sister* Claire wouldn't feel the least bit uncomfortable wearing these.

Claire went to the bathroom once Lesley came back and availed herself of the facilities. It was very quiet and she guessed that everyone had settled down for the night. She sighed as she headed back to their room. All she could do was hope that nobody would question her about what had gone on that night. She wanted to forget it and, most important of all, forget what had triggered that bout of near-hysteria. The less she thought about Jude Slater, the better.

As though thinking about him had conjured him up, he suddenly appeared. It was dark in the corridor with only the light from a single hurricane lantern to lift the gloom and he didn't seem to have seen her. Claire felt her breath catch as he ground to a halt when he spotted her. There was a moment when neither of them moved, when the very air seemed to have stilled, packed so full of thoughts and feelings that it could no longer move. And then Jude took one slow step then another until they were facing each other.

His eyes swept over, burning through the thin cotton of her borrowed pyjamas, scorching her. And even though he didn't say a word Claire knew. She knew what he was thinking. Feeling. She knew because it was what she was thinking and feeling too. He carried on, disappearing into the men's bathroom, but it was several seconds before she could move. She went into her room and lay down on the bed, listening to the hammering of her heart. It knew what had happened, knew and was reacting to it even though she didn't want it to.

Closing her eyes, Claire tried to blot out everything except the thought of sleep but it didn't work. How could it when her body was aching, throbbing, begging for fulfilment? For two whole years the thought of being intimate with a man had been repugnant to her but not any longer. Jude had awoken her dormant emotions and now she felt more vulnerable than ever.

How could she be sure that her mind wouldn't conjure up the memory of that dreadful night if she slept with a man again? That she wouldn't relive the horror of what had happened to her? It had been so hard to put her life back together and find a reason to carry on, and she couldn't do it again. She didn't have the strength. Maybe Jude had aroused feelings she had thought long dead but she couldn't allow them to grow and flourish. It wasn't worth the risk of being plunged back into the abyss.

CHAPTER SIX

A SOFT MIST shrouded the landscape when Jude awoke shortly before six the following morning. He hadn't slept well, and he felt tired and out of sorts as he tossed back the mosquito net and climbed out of bed. Gathering up his wash bag, he made his way to the bathroom, thinking about what had happened the night before.

Meeting Claire in the corridor had been the main reason why sleep had eluded him. Every time he had closed his eyes, he could picture her standing there in those oh-so-prim pyjamas. The women he knew back home wouldn't have been seen dead in an outfit like that but Jude knew that no amount of satin and lace could have had the impact those pyjamas had had on him...

He forced the thought aside as he stepped under the shower. The water was on the cold side of tepid but he preferred it that way. Maybe a cold shower would achieve what all his rationalising had failed to do. Claire wasn't for him, he told himself once more. She wasn't for any man. Her life had been promised to a far higher authority.

By the time he went down for breakfast he felt a little better, more positive about his ability to cope. Maybe he was way out of his comfort zone but he could do this. He only needed to get through the next three months and then he could go back to the life he knew, the comfortable existence he enjoyed...

Did he enjoy it, though? Did he derive any real satisfaction from the luxuries he bought and the expensive restaurants he frequented? Weren't they more a means to compensate himself for doing a job that bored him? Weren't there times when he longed for something more taxing, something that would make a difference to people's lives?

As he helped himself from the breakfast buffet, Jude was suddenly beset by doubts again, and he resented it. Bitterly. Maybe he did want to prove his worth but he hadn't realised it would mean him re-evaluating his whole life!

'Skip the coffee if you value your health.'

Jude glanced round when Matt Kearney called over to him. He nodded when the other man held up a flask and waggled it at him. Picking up his tray, Jude went to join him, forcing himself to smile. Maybe he was starting to have doubts about the life he'd led for the past five years but he would keep them to himself. Pride dictated that he present a confident front.

'I take it that's a tad more palatable than Moses' special brew,' he said lightly as he picked up a mango and started to peel it.

'Too right.' Matt poured a small measure of coffee into a plastic cup that he produced from his canvas holdall. 'Wrap your taste buds round that and see what you think.'

Jude's brows rose as he took a sip. 'Delicious! Where on earth did you get it?'

'Let's just say that I have my sources.' Matt tapped the side of his nose and winked.

Jude laughed. 'In other words, ask no questions and hear no lies.' He took an appreciative swallow of the coffee and sighed. 'I hope you can get some more. I may just survive the next few months with coffee as good as this on tap.'

'I'll do what I can but I can't make any promises.' Matt refilled the cup. 'There's a lot of stuff only available on the black market. Oh, I know we're not supposed to buy from the racketeers but it's part of everyday life over here. If you want something badly enough then you have to pay the going rate for it.'

'Well, I'm more than happy to contribute, although I only have dollars with me, I'm afraid. I was told that it wasn't possible to get hold of the local currency outside the country.'

'That's right. The government put a stop to it being traded but dollars are fine. Folk prefer them, in fact. There's less chance of the dollar being devalued,' he explained when Jude looked questioningly at him.

'Oh, I see. In that case, then, just tell me how much you want.'

'Will do, once I know what my contact is

charging. Prices tend to fluctuate according to demand, if you get my drift.' Matt screwed the lid back on the flask and stood up. 'Right, I'm off to bed. Have a good one.'

'I'll try.'

Jude sketched him a wave and turned back to his breakfast, savouring the sweetly tangy flavour of the mango which tasted so much better than the ones he bought at home. The bread was rather solid and chewy but he made himself eat a whole slice. He didn't want to risk passing out from lack of nourishment, definitely not if he was in Theatre this morning. Why, who knew what he might have to deal with?

The thought of what the day might bring sent a rush of excitement coursing through him. He was smiling as he picked up his tray and took it over to the rack where the dirty dishes were stacked. There were several trays there which meant that most of the others had eaten already. He had better get a move on, he decided. He had no idea what time they were due to be picked up: Claire hadn't told him that.

Bang! That was all it took, just the thought of her and his pulse was off and running again like an Olympic sprinter. As Jude made his way outside, he tried to tell himself that it meant nothing, that it was merely the result of him and Claire having been thrust together into that highly dangerous situation the day before. Why, it was common knowledge that even professional soldiers formed a close bond when they were forced to face untold dangers together, so it was no wonder that he was having all these crazy thoughts after what had gone on.

Jude did his best but no matter how hard he tried to convince himself that was the real explanation, he didn't actually believe it. Somehow, some *way*, Claire had cast a spell over him and no amount of rationalising seemed able to break it.

Claire was relieved when no one mentioned what had gone on the previous night over breakfast. It seemed that everyone had decided to ignore her outburst and she was relieved. Although she knew that folk would be sympathetic if she explained what had caused it, she couldn't bear to go down that route. She didn't want the people she worked with to behave differently around her, to be constantly on their guard in case they said the wrong thing. She just wanted to be treated the same as everyone else.

That was one of the reasons why she hadn't told anyone at the time. It wasn't only what Andrew had said about the police not believing her but the thought of the effect it could have on her family and friends. It had made her see that staying in London was out of the question. Not only would she run the risk of bumping into Andrew but there was also the fear of somehow letting slip about what had happened to her. When the job with the WHO had come up she had immediately applied for it. No matter what dangers she faced, she would feel safer in Mwuranda.

That was why she had decided to stay on when the WHO job had ended. However, the time was fast approaching when she would have to leave. Her visa was due to expire shortly and she couldn't remain in the country without it. The thought of returning to London weighed heavily on her. She had honestly thought that she had turned a corner but what had happened last night had rocked her confidence. Was she really ready to put the past behind her and get on with her life?

Thoughts tumbled around her head as she went outside to wait for the truck. The early morning air was pleasantly cool although the temperature would start to rise soon. All the nurses were wearing cotton scrubs the same as she was wearing. Lesley had lent them to her and Claire was grateful for her kindness. She would miss Lesley and the others when she left Mwuranda. She would miss Jude too.

Her heart lurched even though she knew how stupid it was to think such a thing. She had known him less than a day, so why on earth should she miss him? She tried to dismiss the idea but it wouldn't go away. She was going to miss him whether she liked it or not.

A movement caught her attention and she glanced round, feeling her heart lurch again when she saw Jude standing on the steps. He was wearing khaki chinos and a white T-shirt, and Claire bit her lip. The soft cotton chinos emphasised the muscular length of his legs while the T-shirt highlighted the midnight darkness of his hair. He looked exactly what he was, an incredibly handsome and sexy man in his prime. Even though she didn't want to be aware of him, she couldn't help it.

His eyes suddenly alighted on her and she saw him frown. Striding down the steps, he came straight over to her. 'I thought you were going to rest,' he snapped, his deep voice grating with annoyance.

'I did.' Claire shrugged, hoping that he couldn't tell how keyed up she felt. Now that he was standing right beside her, she could feel the warmth of his skin and smell the citrusy scent of the shower gel he had used that morning. All of a sudden it felt as though her senses were being swamped by him, that he was invading every atom of her being…

'I had a good night's sleep and I feel fine this

morning,' she said, quickly quashing that thought. She wasn't a character in some fifth-rate film. She was a qualified nurse and she knew for a fact that ideas like that were a load of nonsense. Sight, hearing, taste, touch, smell—it needed a lot more than some man's proximity to affect all of them.

'Really? So you're not going to throw another wobble like last night?' Jude folded his arms and regarded her with open scepticism. 'You can swear to that, can you?'

'Yes, I can!' Claire snapped, glaring up at him. Everyone else had had the decency to let matters lie but not him. Oh, no, he had to go raking it all up and make her feel even more unsettled. 'I am perfectly fine, Dr Slater. Thank you for your concern but it is unnecessary, I assure you.'

Fortunately, the truck arrived just then. Claire climbed on board, patting the seat beside her when Lesley followed her inside. Everyone took their places and she was relieved to see that Jude had opted to sit by the tailgate. They set off with a lurch and she grabbed hold of the bench, shaking her head when Lesley apologised as she cannoned into her. It would have been a very different matter, of course, if Jude had been sitting next to her...

Claire erased that thought and concentrated instead on what her friend was saying. Apparently, Lesley had received a letter from her fiancé and wasn't sure what to make of it. She handed it to Claire to see what she thought. Claire's heart sank as she read through the tersely worded paragraphs. Quite frankly, the tone of the letter didn't bode well and she hated to think that her friend might be heading for a major disappointment.

'I've no idea what Tom means about us needing to talk when I get home,' Lesley said as she took the letter back. She frowned. 'I mean, everything's sorted. We've booked the wedding venue and the honeymoon, *and* we've put down a deposit on a house that's being built in an area we both particularly like. What's there to talk about?'

'I don't know,' Claire said carefully. 'You don't think he's having second thoughts, do you?'

'Tom?' Lesley laughed. 'No way! We've been

together since sixth form, so I reckon he knows me inside and out the same as I know him. No, I honestly can't see it's that.'

'Then I have no idea what he wants to talk about.' Claire summoned a smile, not wanting to upset Lesley, hopefully, unnecessarily. 'Mind you, I'm no expert when it comes to relationships. My track record is abysmal.'

'Is that why you're so wary of Jude?' Lesley lowered her voice. 'It's as plain as the nose on my face that he's interested in you, Claire, yet you've batted him into touch in the most effective way possible. No way is he going to try anything now he thinks you're a *nun*!'

'Good. I don't want him trying anything.' She shook her head when Lesley rolled her eyes. 'No. It's true. I'm through with handsome, *charming* men like Jude Slater after what happened the last time.'

'Is that why you've remained over here?' Lesley asked curiously.

'Yes. I got well and truly burnt, and I needed

time to get over it. Being here has helped enormously,' Claire said quietly.

'Helped but not killed off all the demons,' Lesley said astutely. She patted Claire's hand. 'If you ever need a sounding board then you know where I am.'

'I do. Thank you.'

Claire was touched by the offer even though she knew that she would never take Lesley up on it. Her friend let the subject drop and Claire was glad. She didn't want to think about the past, especially now when she felt so vulnerable. She glanced at Jude and sighed. Was he interested in her, as Lesley claimed? She wasn't sure, not that it really mattered because she definitely wasn't going to get involved with him. Maybe she was far more aware of him than she wanted to be but it didn't make any difference. She still wouldn't risk getting involved with anyone after what had happened.

'I'm pleased with his progress, although it will be a while before we can be sure that he's over the worst. In the meantime, I want him kept sedated. It will allow the swelling in his brain to subside and, hopefully, lead to a better outcome.'

Jude handed Ezra's notes to Amy, who was accompanying him on his rounds that morning. Without wanting to appear boastful, he knew that it would be down to his skills as a surgeon if Ezra pulled through. As he followed Amy to the next bed, he felt his spirits lift. He had felt a little deflated after speaking to Claire earlier that morning but this had helped put things into perspective. Even if his reasons for coming to Mwuranda hadn't been as noble as everyone else's, he could still make a positive contribution while he was here.

The rest of the ward round passed quickly. Jude made a couple of minor adjustments to various patients' medication but on the whole he agreed with his colleagues' recommendations. He had been told that there was a clinic that morning which he would be taking, so after he left the ward, he made his way to the main hall where it was being held. He ground to a halt when he saw the queue of people waiting to be seen. He had never imagined there would be this many!

'This way, Dr Slater.'

Jude spun round when he recognised Claire's voice but she had already turned away. He followed her over to where old-fashioned screens had been set up in the corner to form a cubicle. Inside there was an old wooden table—presumably his desk—a couple of equally elderly chairs, plus a battered couch with a trolley beside it holding an ancient sphygmomanometer. Jude's eyes rested on the single piece of equipment. Was this it, then? Was this museum piece the sum total of his diagnostic aids?

He turned to Claire, unable to keep the incredulity out of his voice. 'You must be joking. You surely don't expect me to diagnose patients with only that to help?'

'Of course not.' Claire reached over and opened a drawer in the table. She brought out a stethoscope and offered it to him. 'There's this as well, Dr Slater.'

Jude took the stethoscope off her and stared

at it in disbelief. How could he be expected to function with such a pitiful lack of equipment! Opening his mouth, he started to tell her in no uncertain terms what he thought when he suddenly thought better of it. What would she think if he kicked up a fuss when everyone else simply got on with the job? It was obvious that her opinion of him wasn't all that high and it would only make it sink even further. Was that *really* what he wanted, to be scraping the absolute bottom of the barrel in her eyes?

Jude took a deep breath as he walked around the desk and sat down. Maybe it shouldn't have mattered a jot what Claire thought of him but it did. It mattered a great deal, although he refused to go down the road of wondering why. Looking up, he met her eyes, determined to project an aura of confidence even if his stomach did seem to be suffering from a bad case of the collywobbles.

'If you could show in the first patient, please, Sister. We may as well get started.'

'Of course, Dr Slater.'

There was grudging approval in her voice and

Jude was heartened by it. Maybe he did have his doubts but the fact that Claire approved made him feel much better. He sighed, wondering why she had such an effect on him. It wasn't as though she was going to play a major role in his life, was it? Once he had done his stint here, he wouldn't see her again—their lives were destined to go in completely different directions. For some reason the thought filled him with a deep sense of sadness.

CHAPTER SEVEN

'THIS IS JEREMIAH. He's ten years old and lives at the convent. As you can see, his leg was broken and healed badly, causing problems when he walks.'

Claire ruffled the little boy's black curls. Of all the children the nuns cared for, Jeremiah was her favourite. His parents had been killed when rebel fighters had attacked his village. Although Jeremiah had survived the attack he had been badly injured. His left leg had been broken in several places and as there had been no medical aid available, it had set badly, leaving him with a severe limp. However, he certainly didn't let it slow him down.

'Right. Let's take a look at you, Jeremiah. Can you hop up onto the couch or do you need a lift?'

'I can do it, Mr Doctor.' Jeremiah scrambled onto the couch and sat there beaming happily.

Jude laughed. 'Well done. So let's have a look at this leg and see if there's anything we can do to make it better for you.'

Claire moved aside as Jude donned a pair of gloves and started to examine the child. She had been rather surprised by how well he had got on with their patients. Even though she knew that he was way out of his comfort zone, he had an easy and relaxed manner that people responded to. Now she watched as Jeremiah happily answered his questions. There was more to Jude Slater than she had thought and it was unnerving to admit it. She had to make a conscious effort not to let him see how alarmed she felt when he turned to her.

'Can we get X-rays of his leg? I really need to see how the bone has set before I can determine if there's anything we can do.'

'Of course.' She frowned. 'Sister Anne brought Jeremiah in along with a couple more children from the orphanage. She will need to stay with them, so is it all right if I take him to X-Ray? I can ask Lola to stand in for me,' she added hurriedly.

'I can't see why not.' Jude helped the boy off the bed and smiled at him. 'OK, Jeremiah, you go with Sister Claire and have some pictures taken.'

'Will you be able to make my leg better, Mr Doctor?' Jeremiah asked eagerly. 'So I can play football with the other boys?'

'I don't know.' Jude bent and looked into the child's eyes. 'All I can do is promise that I shall try my very best, but it could turn out that your leg is just too badly damaged.'

Claire heard genuine regret in his voice and once again was surprised. As she led the child out of the cubicle, she couldn't help thinking that Jude was turning out to be very different from what she had thought. Not only did he have a definite rapport with their patients but he genuinely seemed to care about them too. The thought sent a warm little glow through her as she stopped at the office to ask Lola to cover for her. She did her best to ignore it as she accompanied Jeremiah to

Radiography but it proved surprisingly difficult. The fact was that Jude wasn't the self-obsessed individual she had believed him to be and it was worrying to admit it.

Once the X-rays were done, Claire took Jeremiah back to the hall and handed him over to Sister Anne. The X-rays wouldn't be ready until later in the day, so she told the elderly nun that she would arrange for Jeremiah to be seen again later in the week. The rest of the children had been seen by then, so she waved them off and went back to the cubicle. Lola turned and grinned at her when Claire parted the screens.

'Ah, here's *Sister* Claire back again. Right then, I'll leave you two to carry on.'

Claire flushed when Lola winked at her as she left. It was obvious that Lola knew about the misapprehension Jude was under as to her true status and she couldn't help feeling guilty. She busied herself rounding up their next patient, trying not to think about the trick she was playing on him. She wasn't doing it out of a sense of malice, she assured herself, but purely because it made life simpler. If Jude *was* harbouring any ideas about her then it was far more sensible to nip them in the bud than allow them to develop and create a problem.

It was another couple of hours before they finished. It was the middle of the afternoon by then and the temperature inside the hall was stifling. Claire lifted her hair off her neck as she fanned herself with a spare folder. If she didn't get out of here soon, she might very well melt!

'Is it always this hot?' Jude stood up, easing his damp T-shirt away from his body.

Claire hurriedly averted her eyes when she realised that the cotton had turned semi-transparent in places. The sight of all those finely honed muscles visible through the damp fabric made her feel very on edge.

'It's the hottest part of the day,' she replied huskily, then cleared her throat when she saw Jude glance at her. She certainly didn't want him guessing that she had a problem about the way he looked. 'Of course, it doesn't help that we have to hold the clinic in here. There's very little ventilation in the hall despite its size.'

'Couldn't we hold the clinic outside?' Jude suggested. He frowned thoughtfully. 'If we had an awning or something similar then it would make life easier not only for us but for our patients as well. The last thing sick people need is having to wait around in heat like this.'

'It's an idea,' Claire agreed, wondering why no one else had thought of it. They all complained about the heat when they were rostered to work in the clinic and Jude's suggestion could be the solution they needed.

'Do we have such a thing as an awning, do you know?' Jude queried, then grinned at her. 'Or am I hoping for the impossible, like I did before?' He glanced ruefully at the ancient sphygmomanometer and Claire laughed.

'There's more chance of us finding an awning than any modern diagnostic aids,' she told him with a smile.

'Then what are we waiting for?' Jude returned

her smile, his handsome face alight with amusement, and Claire felt her heart skip a beat.

'I've no idea,' she replied, trying to inject a matching lightness into her voice, not the easiest thing to do when her heartbeat was all out of sync. 'If there is anything like that then the only place it can be is in the storeroom round the back. Shall we try there?'

'We most certainly shall.'

Jude pushed open the screen then stood aside for her to lead the way. Claire was conscious of his gaze on her as they left the building. What was he thinking? she mused as they made their way along the path. Was he wondering what they would find in the storeroom or thinking about something else, her perhaps?

She bit her lip as panic assailed her. She didn't want him thinking about her—it was too dangerous. Thoughts led to actions and that was the very thing she wanted to avoid. Something warned her that if Jude ever made a play for her then she might not be able to resist.

* * *

My heaven, but she was lovely!

As Jude followed the slim figure in front of him, he was struck all over again by her beauty. It wasn't just the way she looked but the way she moved. Oh, there was nothing overtly sexual about it; she certainly didn't go in for the artful hip swinging that some women employed. No, it was her natural grace that he admired, the straight line of her back, the set of her shoulders, the way she held her head…

He groaned as his mind went flying off again along routes it wasn't permitted to take. The most disturbing thing of all was that he had never really noticed how a woman walked before. It was as though when he was with Claire he was aware of things that he had never paid any heed to in the past and it scared him. He was getting in way too deep and it had to stop.

'Here we are.'

Claire stopped when they came to some outbuildings and Jude made a determined effort to rein in his thoughts. Claire wasn't for him, he reminded himself, needing to keep that thought at the very forefront of his mind. Stepping forward, he tugged at the rusty old padlock that held the doors together.

'Is there a key for this?' he asked over his shoulder.

'Probably, although I've no idea where it might be.'

Claire stepped forward, bending so she could examine the lock, and Jude sucked in his breath when her shoulder brushed against his. Even though the contact was the most fleeting imaginable, he could feel waves of heat fanning out from where their flesh had connected. It took every scrap of control he could muster not to let her see the effect it had had on him, too.

'In that case, it needs drastic action.' Picking up a stout stick, he pushed it between the hasp and the padlock. A couple of sharp twists and the padlock fell away. He grinned as he kicked it aside. 'Either that lock was completely knackered or I'm stronger than I thought.'

'Hmm. I wonder which it is,' Claire retorted, dryly.

Jude chuckled. It felt remarkably good to be on the receiving end of her teasing, although if anyone else had made fun of him, it would have been a very different story. Once again it was unsettling to realise how differently he behaved when he was with her. He deliberately drove the thought from his mind as he prised open the door. The storeroom was packed from floor to ceiling, the thick layer of dust that coated everything making it impossible to tell what it contained.

'Heaven only knows what's in here,' he said, spluttering a little as he pulled at the edge of a rotting cardboard box, releasing a cloud of dust. 'The whole place will need clearing out before we can see what's what.'

'There's no way we can sort through this lot on our own,' Claire observed with a grimace. 'It will need a whole team of people just to unload all this junk.'

'It will.' Jude huffed out a sigh. 'That knocks my idea on the head, doesn't it?'

'Not necessarily.' She moved aside as he backed out of the storeroom.

Jude raised a questioning brow. 'That sounds as though you have an idea.'

'I was wondering if Matt could come up with something,' she explained. 'Suffice to say that he has his contacts and it's just possible that he might be able to lay his hands on an awning or something similar.'

'Good thinking, Batman!' Jude exclaimed. He grinned at her. 'Shall we go and ask him? We may as well strike while the iron's hot, so to speak.'

'He was on duty last night, so he's not in work today,' she reminded him as they headed back to the hospital.

'Of course. I'll catch him later and see what he says.' He ran his hands over his face to wipe away the perspiration. 'I can't remember ever feeling this hot before.'

'It takes a while to acclimatise,' she agreed then paused. Jude had a feeling that she was debating what she'd been going to say and held his breath because it had to be something important if she was having second thoughts.

'How about a swim to cool you down?' she said finally. She gave a little shrug. 'There's over an hour left before evening ward rounds, so there's plenty of time and it should help to revive you.'

'Sounds great to me,' Jude said huskily. Would Claire join him in the water? he wondered, his heart racing at the thought. He cleared his throat, not wanting her to suspect how much the idea appealed to him. 'Right, which way do we go?'

'Just down here.'

Once again she took the lead only this time Jude refused to let his mind stray even the tiniest bit off course. He couldn't afford to indulge himself when he needed to behave with the utmost propriety. He took a deep breath as they set off through the trees. Claire was placing her trust in him and he wouldn't let her down.

Claire floated on her back, enjoying the sensation of the cool water lapping over her body. Sunlight filtered through the trees and she closed her eyes, letting the play of light and shadow flicker across her eyelids. She could hear the sound of splashing coming from the far side of the pool but she kept her eyes tightly closed. By tacit consent they had each chosen a section of the pool to swim in and she had to admit that she had been relieved. She still wasn't sure it had been a good idea to suggest coming here and it would have been so much worse if they had ended up swimming side by side. The thought of Jude's powerful body so close to hers was far too disturbing.

'This is great!'

Jude's voice carried across to her and Claire reluctantly opened her eyes. He was swimming towards her now, his arms cleaving effortlessly through the water. Sunlight glinted off the droplets of water beading his skin, highlighting the perfectly honed muscles in his arms and shoulders, and she felt her mouth go dry. There was no doubt that the sight of him was having an effect on her.

He laughed when he reached her. 'I may just survive if I can come here and have a dip from time to time. Thank you so much for suggesting it. It was an excellent idea.'

'You're welcome.'

Claire bit her lip when she realised how uptight she sounded but it was hard to respond calmly when he was this close to her. She decided that it might be wiser if she got out of the pool and let her feet drift down to the bottom, but the water was deeper than she had thought. She coughed as she sank beneath the surface and swallowed a mouthful of water.

'Steady!' Jude gripped her arm and drew her safely back to the surface. He looked at her in concern. 'Are you all right?'

'Ye-yes.' She coughed again, trying to expel the water from her lungs, and his grip tightened.

'Don't try to speak. Come on, I'll help you out.' Before Claire realised what was happening, he caught hold of her around the waist and lifted her up onto the bank. Levering himself out of the water, he crouched down beside her. 'Try to relax. The tenser you are, the more difficult it will be to breathe.'

He put his arm around her, obviously trying to encourage her to follow his instructions, but it was impossible. In the absence of anything else, she had opted to swim in the top half of her scrubs. It was something she had done many times before but all of a sudden she was acutely aware of how the wet cotton was clinging to her skin, outlining the curves of her breasts and hips. It was two years since she had been naked in front of a man and even though she wasn't naked now, it felt as though she was. Unbidden her eyes rose to his and she saw the exact moment when concern changed to something else, an emotion that both scared and excited her. To see such naked desire in Jude's eyes was something she wasn't prepared for. When he bent towards her, she didn't move; she just sat there and waited…

'Hey there. Looks like you two have beaten us to it!'

Jude drew back abruptly when Lesley appeared closely followed by the rest of the team. He gave Claire a last searching look and she couldn't fail to see the puzzlement in his eyes before he slid into the water. Claire felt a rush of panic assail her. Was he wondering why she hadn't pushed him away? Why she hadn't given any sign that she didn't welcome his advances? She knew it was true and it was the last thing she wanted. She didn't want to give Jude the wrong impression, certainly didn't want to encourage him, but what had happened just now had shaken her. If they hadn't been interrupted then who knew where it could have led?

'It's a real scorcher of a day, isn't it? Perfect for a dip,' Lesley declared cheerfully as she made her way over to where Claire was sitting. The others had already jumped into the water and Claire was relieved to see that Jude had joined them. She turned to her friend, unable to disguise her anxiety.

'Can I borrow your towel? I didn't bring one with me.'

'Of course.' Lesley handed her the towel, her face filling with concern when she realised how tense Claire looked. 'Are you all right, love? Nothing's happened, has it?' She glanced towards the pool and her mouth thinned. 'Jude didn't try anything, did he?'

'No! Of course not.' Claire forced herself to smile. 'He's been the perfect gentleman.'

'Good. I'm glad to hear it.'

Lesley returned her smile but Claire could tell that her friend was wondering what had upset her. Shaking out the towel, she wrapped it around herself, not wanting to explain why she was so on edge. If she did that then she would have to tell Lesley why she could never have a relationship with Jude and that wasn't an option.

'I think I'll get changed,' she said hurriedly. 'There's a couple of things I need to do before I go off duty but I'll pop back with a dry towel for you.'

'Oh, don't worry about it. I'll borrow Kelly's spare.' Lesley stripped off her scrubs and dropped them on the ground. She was wearing only her underwear beneath, but she didn't let that worry her as she slid into the water. 'See you later,' she called as she set off across the pool to join the others.

Claire watched her for a moment then turned away and headed back to the hospital. How she envied Lesley and the other women, envied their confidence and their self-assurance. One of the worst things about what had happened was the fact that it had made her doubt herself. Had she given out the wrong signals that night? she wondered for the umpteenth time. She had wanted only to end the relationship but was she to blame for what had happened? Had she—as Andrew had claimed—brought it upon herself?

She bit her lip as the old doubts were joined by fresh ones. Had she done the same thing just now, led Jude to think that she had wanted him to touch her, kiss her? She couldn't put her hand on her heart and swear it wasn't true, not when she recalled the effect he'd had on her. Fear rose inside her. It would be so easy to make another mistake. Far too easy with Jude.

CHAPTER EIGHT

JUDE WAS DISAPPOINTED to find that Claire wasn't in the dining room when he went down for dinner. He hadn't seen her since she had left the pool and he had been hoping that she would be there that night. Jeremiah's X-rays had come back and he wanted to discuss them with her—or that was what he had told himself. It had seemed safer than admitting that he desperately wanted to see her.

Jude sighed as he went to the serving hatch. He had come so close to crossing the line today. If they hadn't been interrupted then he knew that he would have kissed her. He felt guilty as hell about it, too, and yet he couldn't rid himself of the thought that Claire might not have spurned his advances. Even though he knew it was madness, he couldn't get the idea out of his head.

144 REAWAKENED BY THE SURGEON'S TOUCH

After all, she must have known what was about
to happen, so why hadn't she stopped him? Why
had she sat there, looking at him? It didn't make
sense which was why he needed to speak to her.
He mentioned her absence to Lesley as they carried their plates back to the table.

'What's happened to Claire tonight?' he said,
deliberately keeping his tone light.

'She's gone back to the convent,' Lesley explained as they sat down. 'Apparently, the nuns
have found some old cartoons and they're plan-
ning to show them to the kids tonight as a treat.'

'Oh, I see.' Jude dredged up a smile. He certainly didn't want Lesley guessing how disappointed he felt. That would only lead to questions
and that was the last thing he wanted. 'Well, I'm
sure the children will enjoy them. They've been
through such a lot, from what I can gather. They
deserve a bit of fun.'

'They do indeed.' Lesley forked up a mouthful of rice. She chewed and swallowed it then
looked at him. 'Nothing happened today at the
pool, did it?'

'Such as?' Jude said, feigning surprise although his heart had started pounding.

'I don't know. That's why I'm asking you. Only Claire seemed very…well, *uptight*, for want of a better word. I wondered if you two had fallen out about something.'

'No, of course not!' Jude exclaimed in dismay. 'Why? Did Claire say that we had?'

'No. On the contrary, she said you'd been the perfect gentleman.' Lesley sighed. 'Take no notice. It's just that she seemed very tense earlier on and I was wondering if there was a reason for it.'

'And you've no idea what was wrong with her?' Jude asked, overwhelmed by guilt. Had he completely misread the situation? Far from being receptive, had Claire been upset by what had so nearly happened?

'None at all. I love Claire to bits. She's one of the sweetest, kindest people I know, but she doesn't give much away. I know nothing about her past life, for instance, apart from the fact that she was working in London before she came out

here.' Lesley grimaced. 'Still, we all have our se-
crets. I'm just being a nosy old bag!'

Jude laughed as he was expected to do but he
couldn't deny that he felt dreadful. The thought
that he had upset Claire was more than he could
bear. He wanted to improve her opinion of him,
not make it any worse!

They were halfway through the film show when
five-year-old Bebe started crying and clutching
her stomach. Claire hurriedly got up and went
to her. Crouching down, she laid her hand on
the child's forehead and was dismayed to dis-
cover how hot she felt. When Sister Anne came
to see what was happening, Claire told her that
she would take the little girl to the sick bay. She
got Bebe settled in a bed and examined her. It
was immediately apparent that the child was in
a great deal of pain; she started screaming when
Claire gently palpated her abdomen.

'Shh, sweetheart. I'm sorry. I didn't mean to
hurt you.'

Claire stroked the little girl's cheek but she had

to admit that she was extremely concerned. Although it wasn't possible to make a conclusive diagnosis, Bebe was exhibiting all the symptoms of appendicitis, and if that were the case then she needed to be seen immediately by a doctor. When Sister Julie came to see what was happening, Claire explained her concerns to her.

'So what do you suggest, Claire?' Sister Julie asked anxiously. 'Shall we try to get hold of a driver and take her to the hospital?'

'I think it would be far too much for her,' Claire replied, glancing at the little girl. 'She's in tremendous pain and being jolted over all those potholes will only make matters worse. No, we need to get one of the doctors to come here and see her.'

'In that case I shall radio the hospital and see what they can arrange.'

Sister Julie hurried away, leaving Claire to watch over the child. She fetched a bowl of tepid water and gently sponged Bebe's face and neck. The child's high temperature worried her most of all as it could signify that her appendix had perforated and that peritonitis had set in, and that was extremely serious. It was a relief when she heard footsteps coming along the corridor some time later, heralding the arrival of one of the doctors from the Worlds Together team.

Claire straightened up, the welcoming smile freezing on her lips when Jude followed Sister Julie into the room. For some reason she hadn't expected him to respond to their call for assistance and it threw her completely off balance to see him standing there. In a fast sweep, her eyes travelled from the top of his gleaming black hair to the tips of his expensively shod feet and she only just managed to bite back her groan as another image promptly superimposed itself on the reality before her. Now all she could see was Jude as he had looked that afternoon, his powerful body gleaming with moisture as he had sat on the edge of the pool, looking at her with such hunger in his eyes.

Her breath caught because she knew it was an image that was going to stay with her for a long time to come.

* * *

'There's a strong chance her appendix has perforated.'

Jude moved away from the bed and went over to the sink to wash his hands. He glanced round, doing his best to contain his feelings when Claire remained at the child's bedside. Maybe he should put it down to concern for their patient; however, he suspected there was a very different reason why she appeared so keen to maintain her distance from him. Once again he felt a rush of guilt rise up inside him so that it was an effort to concentrate when she spoke.

'I did wonder if it might be that with her running such a high temperature.'

Her voice was cool, in keeping with her overall demeanour since he had arrived, and Jude sighed. If he had upset her then he wished to heaven that she would come out and say so. Treating him with this icy politeness only made him feel worse!

'If peritonitis has set in then her temperature will be elevated,' he replied gruffly. He dried his hands and went back to the bed, taking care not to encroach on her personal space. He'd committed enough sins for one day! 'I'll need to operate immediately and see what's going on. If her appendix has ruptured, the longer the delay, the worse the outcome will be. Is there anywhere suitable here at the convent or will we need to transfer her to hospital? I'd like to avoid that if it's possible,' he added.

'Actually, the convent used to have its own hospital. Apparently, the nuns used to run it before the uprising. It was closed then but I know there was an operating theatre,' Claire explained then grimaced. 'However, it's not been used for years, so I've no idea what state it's in.'

'Then we'd better go and take a look.' Jude raised his brows when she failed to move. 'If you could show me the way, please, Sister?'

'Oh! Yes. Of course.'

A touch of colour stained her cheeks as she hurriedly led the way from the room. Jude forbore to say anything as he followed her along the corridor, but her reluctance to be around him was going to make life extremely difficult in the coming weeks. Although he appreciated why she was behaving this way, he couldn't help wondering why she hadn't made her feelings clearer that afternoon. If she had given him even the tiniest hint that she had felt uncomfortable then he would never have let things go that far. Once again the thought that there was something odd about her behaviour rose to his mind but he blanked it out. He wasn't going to complicate matters even further by going down that route again.

Claire stopped when they reached a set of double doors. Pushing open one of the doors, she felt for the light switch. 'I hope the lights still work,' she murmured.

Jude stepped inside when the lights came on, turning in a slow circle as he took stock. Although the equipment was dated, there appeared to be everything there they needed. The other plus point was that the whole place was spotlessly clean. 'This is fine,' he declared. 'I've brought my case with me, so we just need to make sure that the operating table and anaesthetic equipment are sterile before we start.'

He glanced at Claire, keeping his face free of expression. Maybe he was puzzled by her behaviour but it would be better to leave things how they were rather than go raking it all up. He didn't want to embarrass her and he certainly didn't want to explain why *he* had acted the way he had done. Heat ran through him at the thought of admitting how much he had wanted to kiss her. It was out of the question to do that.

'Have you anaesthetised a patient before?' he asked, deliberately focusing on the task at hand.

'Yes. Bill showed me what to do, although it was only the once when he wasn't feeling well. I'm certainly no expert,' she added quietly.

'So long as you understand the basics,' Jude replied curtly. 'However, if you're tied up doing that then I'll need someone else to assist me. Would one of the sisters be able to help, do you think?'

'I'm not sure.' She frowned as she considered the question and Jude's hands clenched. All of a sudden he was overwhelmed by the urge to smooth away those tiny lines marring her brow. It took every scrap of willpower he could muster not to give in to it.

'Sister Julie used to be a nurse—I remember her mentioning that she worked at St. Linus's Hospital in London, although I've no idea which department she was in.'

She looked up and Jude hurriedly adopted a noncommittal expression. The thought of running his fingertips over her brow was giving him hot and cold chills and it was alarming to realise how out of character he was behaving. He had dated many beautiful women over the years, not only dated them either but slept with them as well. However, he couldn't remember ever feeling this aroused before.

'Perhaps you could ask her if she would assist me,' he suggested, his voice grating. He saw Claire glance at him but thankfully she didn't say anything before she left.

Jude went to check on Bebe again, doing his best to ignore all the crazy feelings rushing around inside him. He had sworn after his experiences five years ago that he would never allow himself to become emotionally involved again but it was different with Claire—he couldn't seem to detach himself as he usually did. She wasn't for him; she never could be his, he reminded himself. But even though his mind understood that rock-solid, his heart refused to believe it. He sighed wearily. Maybe it was being here that was causing the problem. He was so far out of his comfort zone that everything was all mixed up: his thoughts, his feelings, what he wanted from life; every single thing. Once he was back in England it would be a different story. He would pick up the threads and carry on as before.

He frowned as he looked at the little girl lying in the bed. Once again the thought of continuing to live his life the way he had been doing held very little appeal. He had a feeling that nothing would be the same ever again.

Sister Julie agreed to help, so in a very short time the operation went ahead. Once Jude was satisfied that Bebe was properly anaesthetised he made an incision in her abdomen. Claire gasped because it was immediately apparent what had happened. Although the appendix had perforated, the infection had been contained by the omentum—the fold of membrane that hangs in front of the intestines. This had stuck to the appendix and formed an abscess which was why the little girl had been in such pain.

'She'll need antibiotics before I can risk draining this abscess and removing the appendix,' Jude declared. He looked at Claire over his mask and she could see the concern in his eyes. 'She's a very sick little girl and the outcome is by no means guaranteed.'

Claire nodded although she didn't say anything. The thought of the child's life being at risk after everything she had been through had brought a lump to her throat and she didn't want Jude to know how emotional she felt. For some reason she knew it would make her feel even more vulnerable.

They returned Bebe to the sick bay. Fortunately, Jude had brought antibiotics with him, so Claire set up a drip, although she suspected that the little girl would need something stronger to deal with the infection. She wasn't surprised when Jude announced that he intended to transfer Bebe to hospital as soon as possible.

'Can it wait until the morning?' Claire asked as she finished taping the cannula to Bebe's arm. She sighed when she saw him frown. 'I know how important it is to get the correct antibiotics into her, but it's too risky to drive into town at this time of the night. If it can wait till daylight, it will be much safer.'

'I suppose so,' he agreed with marked reluctance. 'But I'd like to leave at first light. The sooner we get the antibiotics sorted, the better her chances will be.'

'Of course.' Claire moved away from the bed, her breath catching when her hand accidentally brushed against his arm. She could feel the silky-soft hair on his forearm tickling her skin and swallowed as she was beset by a sudden rush of awareness. She hurried to the door, desperate to put some space between them. The last thing she needed was to be even more aware of him than she already was.

'I'll get onto Lola and make arrangements for Bebe to be moved in the morning,' she said, over her shoulder.

'Thank you.' There was something in his voice that made her heart race. Had he felt it too? Felt that flash of awareness that had passed through her? Common sense decreed it was impossible, that no one could experience another person's feelings, yet she couldn't dismiss the idea.

'I take it that I'll be staying here for the night.'

There was nothing in his voice to alarm her now, yet Claire still hesitated before she turned. Had she been mistaken? she wondered. Imagined something that simply hadn't happened? She searched his face and found her answer in the brooding intensity of his gaze. Her breath caught. She hadn't imagined it. Jude was every bit as aware of her as she was of him and it made the situation even more dangerous.

'Yes. I...I'll sort out a room you can use,' she said quickly, struggling to hold on to her composure. 'With all the children being here there isn't a lot of free space, but I'm sure we can find somewhere for you to sleep.'

'Don't go to any trouble,' he said quietly. 'I'll sleep in here if there's nowhere else. In fact, it might be better if I did. I can keep an eye on Bebe then. She is one very sick little girl.'

The concern on his face as he looked at the child was unmistakable. Claire felt a rush of warmth run through her. There was no doubt that Jude cared deeply about their small patient and it simply proved that her initial impression of him had been completely wrong. As she left the room, she suddenly found herself wondering if she should rectify the mistake he had made about her. Surely he deserved to know that she wasn't a nun? It didn't seem fair to let him carry on believing it and yet if she did tell him the truth, it could have repercussions.

She bit her lip as panic rose inside her. Recalling what had so nearly happened at the pool that afternoon, not to mention what had gone on just now, was it really wise to remove the final

barrier between them? Maybe she did feel differently about him, but it didn't mean that she
could cope with having a relationship with him.

CHAPTER NINE

MORNING DAWNED, CALM and clear, such a contrast to his state of mind that Jude found it hard to believe a new day had begun with so little fanfare. He had spent the night going over what had happened the evening before. Oh, he had tried to convince himself that he'd been mistaken, that Claire *hadn't* reacted to his touch, but he had failed. Miserably. Hadn't he felt that flash of awareness that had passed between them? Experienced that charge of electricity that had filled the air? Of course he had and there was no point trying to deny it either! Coming on top of what had gone on earlier at the pool, it was little wonder that he felt so confused.

He got out of bed and went to the window, resting his forehead against the glass as he went over it all once more. Why should Claire be attracted to him when she had sworn to forgo the pleasures of the flesh? Last night his thoughts had been in such turmoil that it had been impossible to think clearly, but he needed to set aside his own feelings if he was to make sense of it all. It was what he was good at, after all; disregarding emotions and rationalising a problem had always been his forte. With a bit of luck it would work this time too.

Jude wasn't sure how long he stood there, trying to work out the answer to this particular puzzle, but the sun had risen above the horizon when he finally gave up. Maybe Claire had had her reasons but he couldn't explain them. That was certain.

He checked on Bebe, as he had done many times during the night. Although her condition hadn't changed very much, her temperature was slightly lower than it had been, which was encouraging. When Sister Anne came to relieve him, he made his way to the dining room, pausing in the doorway while he took in the scene that greeted him. There appeared to be children everywhere, some seated at tables, others sitting cross-legged on the floor. Every child had a bowl in front of him or her and every single one was tucking in to their breakfast. How the nuns had managed to get them all served was a miracle to his mind, but even the very smallest—little more than babies—were eating.

He spotted Claire at the far side of the room, helping a tiny tot scoop up cereal with a spoon. Jude felt a rush of emotion hit him as he watched her wipe the little one's mouth then drop a kiss on the child's upturned face. There was such tenderness in the gesture, such loving care, that he couldn't help feeling envious.

'Ah, Dr Slater. Good morning. Do come and join us.'

Jude swung round when Sister Julie materialised beside him. 'Good morning, Sister,' he replied then cleared his throat when he realised how choked he sounded. Deliberately, he turned so that he could no longer see Claire. Feeling jealous of a child really was beyond the pale!

'I hope you slept well,' Sister Julie continued as she led him over to where an elderly nun was serving breakfast.

'Very well, thank you,' Jude replied, deeming it wiser not to admit to his sleepless night, let alone the reason for it. Heat rushed through him and he hurried on. 'Mealtimes must be very busy times for you.'

'They are indeed.' Sister Julie treated him to a gentle smile. 'Food is extremely important to the children. Most of them have gone hungry in their short lives and they attach huge importance to being fed.' She gestured towards the stack of empty bowls. 'As you can see, nothing is wasted. When you grow up not knowing where your next meal is coming from then you eat every scrap.'

'I see,' Jude said quietly. Oh, he had seen the appeals on television, even donated to them on many an occasion, but that was very different from witnessing the effects of poverty at first hand. He couldn't help feeling guilty about all the times he had turned up his nose at some perfectly good meal simply because it hadn't tempted his palate.

'There is no need to berate yourself, Dr Slater. None of us can fully comprehend what it must be like to go without food unless we have experienced it for ourselves.' Sister Julie smiled sympathetically. 'It hit me hard when I first came here too.'

'It makes me feel very guilty,' Jude admitted, even though he was surprised that he should open up to such an extent. He never discussed his feelings and yet here he was, admitting that he was ashamed of the way he had taken his good fortune for granted.

'It does.' Sister Julie looked calmly back at him. 'I found the best antidote for my guilt was to do something to help.'

She didn't say anything else as she filled a bowl with porridge and handed it to him. Jude took it over to a table and sat down, mulling over what he had heard. Dipping his spoon into the bowl, he tried a little of the cereal. It tasted very gritty and at any other time he would have left it, but he ate every scrap. How could he waste it after hearing about all these children who had gone hungry?

All of a sudden he was filled with a fresh resolve. Maybe he had come to Mwuranda for the sake of his pride but it didn't mean he couldn't help the people of this country. And not just while he was here either: he could help when he returned home by fundraising. He knew a lot of wealthy people and if he could get them to contribute then there was no end to the good they could do…

Was it only because he wanted to improve people's lives? a small voice suddenly whispered in his ear. *Or was there another reason?*

Jude's gaze went to Claire and he sighed. He couldn't put his hand on his heart and swear that his reasons for wanting to help were purely altruistic. The fact that it might improve his standing in Claire's eyes had a lot to do with it, even though he knew how pointless it was. No matter if he raised his status to sainthood level, Claire could never be his.

* * *

The ambulance arrived shortly before seven a.m. Claire helped to load Bebe on board then climbed in beside her. Jude was having a word with the driver before they set off and she shivered as she listened to him instructing the man to drive carefully and avoid the potholes. Far too many times during the night her sleep had resounded to the sound of that deep voice. It was as though it had imprinted itself in her mind and, try as she may, she couldn't shift it.

'Right. Let's hope we don't encounter the kind of problems we did when I arrived.'

Jude climbed in and slammed the door. Claire summoned a smile, not wanting him to suspect how on edge she felt. It wasn't just the sound of his voice that had disturbed her sleep but everything else that had happened yesterday—the incident at the pool, that flash of awareness that had passed between them. Heat flowed through her and it took every scrap of control she could muster not to betray how alarmed she felt.

'Hopefully, we'll have an uneventful journey today,' she murmured.

'Amen to that,' Jude replied, drolly, then grimaced. 'Sorry. No disrespect meant.'

Claire nodded, feeling infinitely guilty that he had felt it necessary to apologise. She turned away, checking Bebe's obs to give herself time to collect herself. Even though she felt bad about misleading him, surely it was better than telling him the truth? The fact that she was so vulnerable where Jude was concerned was worrying enough, but the fact that he obviously felt something for her made it even more dangerous. How could she hope to do the sensible thing if she had to contend with his feelings as well as her own?

The thought occupied her for the rest of the journey. It was a relief when the ambulance drew up outside the hospital. Jude and the driver lifted the stretcher out of the back and carried it inside. Claire led the way to a side room which was kept for emergency cases like this. Bebe would need intensive nursing and it would make it easier if she wasn't in a ward with all the usual comings and goings.

Following local tradition, the Mwurandan people were cared for by their relatives while they were in hospital and it could be extremely noisy at times with so many people milling about. Although they had tried to instigate a *'no more than two people at a bed'* rule, it was rarely observed. Mothers, fathers, wives, husbands, aunts, uncles, cousins—the list was endless. At least Bebe would have some peace and quiet in the side room.

Claire made the child comfortable then went to the office to sign in. Lola grinned at her when she opened the door. 'Ah, so you made it back safely. I hope you brought Jude with you? I had visions of you leaving him at the convent!'

'Of course he's come back with me,' Claire said sharply then sighed. 'Sorry. I didn't mean to snap at you.'

'No sweat, honey. I should know better than to tease you about such a touchy subject.'

Claire flushed. 'There's nothing touchy about it.'

'No? My mistake.'

Lola tactfully let the subject drop but Claire was very aware that she had handled things badly. Just for a moment she found herself wondering if it would be simpler to tell Lola why she was so edgy around Jude before she thought better of it. Her hand shook as she signed her name on the sheet. It was the first time that she had been seriously tempted to tell anyone about her past but she was afraid that she would regret it. The problem was that she had no idea how people would react and she hated to think that they might view her in a different light afterwards.

Her breath caught as an even worse thought occurred to her. How would *Jude* react if he found out that she had been raped? At the moment he thought she was a nun and he probably conformed to most people's view of the women who had chosen that kind of a life. It would come as a massive shock if he discovered that she wasn't the innocent he believed her to be.

Tears welled to her eyes. She couldn't bear to imagine his reaction if he found out he was wrong.

It was late afternoon before there was any real change in Bebe's condition. Jude checked her chart, relieved to see that there was a definite improvement in her obs. He had to admit that he had been extremely concerned about having to delay the operation to remove her appendix. Although the circumstances were very different, he couldn't help thinking about Maddie and how delaying her surgery had had such disastrous consequences. However, it appeared that the broad-spec antibiotics he had prescribed were doing their job.

'Definitely an improvement, although it will be at least another day before I can risk operating.' He handed the chart to Claire, automatically batting it down when his pulse gave a familiar leap as their hands touched. He had done his best to avoid her, needing a break from all the soul-searching he had been doing lately. Maybe that was the key, he had decided: steer clear of her. From the moment he had arrived in Mwuranda they had been thrust together, but if he kept out of her way then surely he would get back on track.

In truth, he had never spent so much time with *any* woman before. Dates were usually confined to dinner and possibly a show beforehand. If he and his date ended up in bed then it was always at the woman's home too. It meant he could leave afterwards and not have to spend the night with her. He had never lived with anyone, never been tempted to forfeit his single life...

Up till now.

Jude's heart plummeted. It plunged right down to his boots then surged back up again so fast that he felt light-headed. Love. Marriage. Home. Family. They were mere words to him, words other people used and ones he avoided. He had no interest in exploring any of those options, had no desire to be a husband or a father or anything else that involved commitment. Oh, he had nothing against marriage per se but it wasn't for him. He had seen too many marriages end in disaster to go down that route, starting with his own parents.

A shudder ran through him as he recalled when his parents had split up. Although he had been only seven when they had divorced, he had recognised the hatred in their voices whenever they had spoken to each other. It had been a relief when he was sent away to boarding school, in fact. Unlike the other new boys he hadn't been homesick. He had been glad to be there, well away from those hate-filled voices. Although he had spent holidays with both his mother and his father after the divorce, he had never missed them when it had been time to return to school. School had had rules and regulations—he had felt safe there well away from all the emotional turmoil.

It was only after he had qualified that he had started to feel anything. Helping the people who had come to him had unlocked his emotions; he had found himself empathising with them. It had been Maddie's death that had made him see how stupid he was. Allowing himself to care about other people always ended in heartache—his parents, Maddie, Claire.

Panic ripped through him and he turned away, afraid that Claire would pick up on his mood. 'We'll continue with the antibiotics,' he said brusquely. 'We may need to change them but I'll decide that when the cultures come back.'

'Should we continue with twenty-minute obs?' Claire asked and the very coolness of her tone told him that she had recognised his change of mood even if she didn't understand the reason for it.

'Of course.' He stared aloofly back at her, opting for a technique he employed whenever he was dealing with a particularly obtuse colleague. Maybe it was unfair to use it now but it was better than letting her know how he really felt, how afraid he was. 'As I said, Sister, it could be another twenty-four hours before I can risk operating. None of us can afford to be less than vigilant during that time, including you.'

'Of course.'

Her tone was just as cool but he could tell that

his sharp reply had hurt her. Jude felt like the lowest form of life as he left the room. The urge to go back and apologise was overwhelming but he forced himself to carry on, making his way to the office to sign out. He had to be strong. He couldn't allow his emotions to get the better of him. Even if he had been thinking about making a commitment, it wouldn't be to Claire. Her future was mapped out and, oddly enough, it was very similar to his own.

Like him, Claire wouldn't fall in love, she wouldn't get married, she wouldn't have children. She would dedicate her life to following her vocation. Even though Jude knew that she was doing exactly what she wanted, he couldn't help feeling wretched at the thought of everything she was giving up. Someone as sweet and as gentle, as kind and as beautiful as Claire deserved so much more.

CHAPTER TEN

CLAIRE DECIDED TO stay the night at the hospital so she would be on hand if there was a deterioration in Bebe's condition. Although she knew the night staff would take good care of the little girl, she wanted to be there in case anything happened. Jude's parting comment had stung and she had no intention of giving him another opportunity to take her to task. Bill Arnold was duty doctor that night and he helped her move a chair into the side room.

'Are you sure about this?' he asked, his kindly face mirroring concern as they placed the chair beside the bed. 'I mean, you were working all day and it seems a bit much to expect you to work through the night as well.'

'I don't mind.' Claire summoned a smile, not wanting the older man to guess why she felt it necessary to stay. Admitting that it had been Jude's wholly unjustified rebuke that had made her decide not to leave would be tantamount to admitting that she cared what he thought. And that was the last thing she intended to do.

'Well, make sure you get some sleep. You'll be neither use nor ornament tomorrow if you're tired out.'

Bill patted her hand and left. Claire busied herself with Bebe's obs, noting them down on the chart with even more care than usual. No way was Jude going to find anything to complain about!

She sighed as she hung the chart on the end of the bed. She knew she was overreacting but she couldn't help it. It was as though every fibre of her being was attuned to his mood. If he was happy, she felt happy, and if he was annoyed, she felt unsettled too. Bearing in mind that they had met only days ago, it was hard to believe that he could have this effect on her, but there was no point pretending. Jude made her feel things she had never expected to feel. The key now was to learn how to moderate her response before it caused a problem—if it hadn't already done so.

Heat rushed through her as she recalled what had happened the day before. She had never expected to feel desire again after what had happened to her, but that was what she had felt, an all-encompassing need to touch Jude and have him touch her. Even now she could feel the echo of it resonating deep inside her and it scared her. How could she risk giving herself to a man again? How could she be sure that he wouldn't hurt her? The old fear might have faded but it hadn't gone away; it was still there, a dark shadow at the back of her mind.

She took a deep breath but the facts had to be faced. She couldn't be sure that it wouldn't rear up and destroy her life all over again.

Jude was first in the dining room for breakfast the following morning. Another restless night had left him feeling drained. He had kept harking back to how Claire had sounded when he had left her the previous day. He knew he had upset her and he felt guilty about it too. Just because he was worried about getting involved, it wasn't an excuse to speak to her the way he had done and as soon as he saw her, he would apologise. Even if he did intend to steer clear of her in the future, it was the very least he could do.

His heart was heavy as he went to the buffet. When Moses offered him some of his specially brewed coffee, he accepted that too. Not quite the traditional hair shirt worn by the penitent but it would have much the same effect! He had just sat down when Bill Arnold appeared.

'Another early bird,' the older man observed as he loaded a plate with fruit. He added a hunk of bread and carried the whole lot over to the table and sat down. 'I don't know how you young 'uns do it. Matt turned up way before he was supposed to do, which is why I finished early. And Claire couldn't have had more than an hour's sleep last night, but there she was this morning, rushing around all over the place.'

'Claire's already at the hospital!' Jude exclaimed in surprise.

'She stayed the night there.' Bill broke off a chunk of bread and smothered it in some of the locally produced jam. Jude waited impatiently while he chewed it. 'I assumed you knew she was staying over.'

'No. I had no idea,' Jude replied, frowning. 'Did she say why she had decided to stay?'

'No. But she was with Bebe all night, so I assume she wanted to keep an eye on her. Typical of Claire. She always puts everyone else before herself.'

Bill carried on eating, obviously keen to get finished so that he could take himself off to bed. No wonder, Jude thought as the older man departed a few minutes later. Working twelve-hour shifts was exhausting enough and doubly so under these conditions. It made Claire's decision to work a double shift all the more difficult to understand—unless it was his comments that had spurred her into it.

The thought that he was responsible hit him hard. Jude stood up and carried his tray over to the rack even though he had barely touched his breakfast. Leaving the dining room, he hurried outside and made his way round to the rear of the building. One of the drivers had recovered the motorbike Claire had used to collect him from the airport and it was stored in the shed back there.

Jude wheeled it out, relieved to find that the key was in the ignition. He fired up the engine, grimacing as ancient pistons struggled to find some kind of rhythm. It was years since he had ridden a motorbike and it had been a modern version too, nothing like this heap of old junk, but he had no intention of letting that deter him. He needed to apologise to Claire and he needed to do it soon.

Claire had just finished sponging Bebe's face when the door opened. She glanced round, expecting it to be one of the local nurses coming to see if she needed help. The polite refusal was already hovering on her lips when she discovered that it was Jude.

'What are you doing here?' she demanded, unable to hide her dismay. 'The day staff isn't due for another half hour at least.'

'I wanted a word with you, so I came on ahead.'

He came into the room and closed the door. Claire shivered when she saw how grim he looked. Surely he didn't still believe that she was incapable of looking after Bebe properly, did he? The thought was like the proverbial red rag and Claire rounded on him, her grey eyes spitting sparks. Maybe she wouldn't have reacted so forcefully if she hadn't been so tired after working a double shift, but any thoughts of moderating her response flew straight out of the window as she let rip.

'Oh, did you? And what exactly did you want a word with me about? Or do I really need to ask that question?' She laughed bitterly. 'You made your feelings about my competence perfectly clear, Dr Slater, so I can only assume that you wish to take me to task once more. So come along, then. How have I failed to meet your exacting standards this time?'

'I haven't come here to take you to task,' he replied harshly. 'If you want the truth then I came to apologise, but obviously it would be a waste of my time as well as yours.'

He went to leave but there was no way that Claire was prepared to let him off so lightly. His scathing comment had hurt and she wasn't going to let him brush it aside with some trumped-up claim about apologising. From what she had learned, Jude Slater didn't go in for apologies. For any reason. To anyone!

She caught hold of his arm as he went to open the door. He was wearing a short-sleeved shirt and his flesh felt warm to her touch, warm and wonderfully vital. Claire had the craziest feeling that she could actually feel his life force pulsating beneath her fingers and it shook her. She had never felt this connection to anyone before, never experienced this feeling that she was within a hair's breadth of touching the very essence of another human being. It was a moment of such profundity that it cut right through her anger. Now all she felt was a deep sense of hurt. How could Jude believe that she wasn't up to doing her job?

Even if he knew nothing else about her, surely he could tell how much her work meant to her, that it was the one thing that had given her life any meaning?

Tears blurred her vision and she let her hand fall from his arm. She'd had years of practice at containing her emotions yet she couldn't seem to contain them any longer. It was as though all the pain and heartache that had built up inside her was gushing out in an unstoppable tide.

'Here. Sit down.'

Jude's touch was infinitely gentle as he led her to the chair, his voice filled with compassion, and it just made everything worse. Anger would have been better, she thought wretchedly as she sank down onto the cushion. She could have coped with his anger; it would have firmed her resolve and helped her pull herself together. However, gentleness and compassion were very different emotions. They slid past her defences and found all the vulnerable places that she kept hidden.

'Don't cry, Claire. Please!' He knelt in front of her and she couldn't fail to see the anguish on his face. 'I can't bear to know you're so unhappy and that it's all my fault. I never meant to upset you. Truly I didn't. I don't have any doubts whatsoever about your competence.'

'Then why did you say what you did?' she said brokenly.

'Because I was upset.'

'Upset!' she exclaimed in surprise. She took a shuddery breath as she wiped her eyes with the back of her hand. 'Upset because of something I'd done, you mean?'

'No.' He hesitated, giving her the distinct impression that he was reluctant to explain. When he finally spoke, his voice was rough with emotion. 'I had a patient once, a young girl several years older than Bebe, who died after I had to delay operating on her. I…well, I couldn't help thinking about her and that's why I spoke to you so sharply. But you must believe me when I say that I have every confidence in you. You are a superb nurse.'

There was no doubt in her mind that he was telling her the truth and Claire felt her eyes fill with tears once more. The fact that he cared enough to talk about something that obviously distressed him touched her deeply. It was so long since anyone had considered her feelings that she was overwhelmed. Tears began to stream down her face again and she heard him sigh.

'I'm so sorry, Claire. You're the last person I wanted to hurt. Please forgive me.' Leaning forward, he gathered her into his arms. His body felt warm and hard as she rested against him, indubitably male too, but oddly that didn't worry her as she might have expected. Jude wouldn't hurt her. She could trust him.

Whether it was that thought which destroyed the final line of her defence, she wasn't sure, but she nestled against him, letting his strength fill her with an inner peace she hadn't felt in a very long time. Ever since the night she had been raped she had been running: away from Andrew; away from what had happened; away from herself. Far too often she had found herself wondering if she could have done something to prevent the attack, but not any longer. Now she could see that *she* wasn't to blame, that *she* had done nothing wrong, that *she* was the victim. And knowing it set her free.

Jude could sense a shift in the mood even though he didn't understand what had caused it. Claire didn't say anything but he felt the tension start to ease from her body. His breath caught when she settled against him so trustingly. He had wanted only to comfort her, yet all of a sudden he was filled with a sense of wonder. Holding her in his arms, feeling her heart beating in time with his, felt so right!

'Claire.' Her name was the faintest murmur, barely disturbing the air between them as he bent towards her. His mind was awash with so many emotions that he couldn't have put a name to even half of them. All he knew was that everything he felt seemed to be condensed into this single moment…

'I think Claire's in here. I'll go and see.' The sound of voices in the corridor broke the spell.

Jude shot to his feet just a second before the door opened and Matt appeared.

'There's a phone call for you, Claire,' he announced cheerfully. 'Oh, hi, Jude. I didn't know you were in here. Anyway, it's Sister Julie. She wants to know how Bebe's doing.'

'I…I'll be right there.'

Claire stood up as Matt disappeared and Jude could see that she was trembling. She didn't look at him as she went to the door but there was no way that he could let her leave like this, he realised sickly. He had come so close to compromising her beliefs and making a mockery of everything she stood for. Apologising couldn't begin to make up for what he had done, but it was the only option open to him.

'I'm sorry. I didn't mean to embarrass you. I just wanted to…well, comfort you.'

'I know.' She gave him a tight little smile and left.

Jude followed her from the room and made his way outside. He stood on the steps, feeling his insides quivering as reaction set in. He felt guilty as hell about what he had done, but underneath it there was a deep sense of sadness, of loss. He would never make love to Claire, never experience the joy and fulfilment of their bodies becoming one. Sex had been little more than a mechanical process for him up till now, enjoyable enough but not exactly meaningful. However, he realised that it would have been far more than that with Claire. His mind as well as his body would have been engaged if he'd had the chance to love her, as he would never do. Tears suddenly blurred his vision. The future had never seemed bleaker.

CHAPTER ELEVEN

CLAIRE CAST A final glance in the mirror. It was Bill's sixty-fifth birthday and the team had decided to throw a party for him that night to celebrate. Moses had been enlisted to bake him a birthday cake and there was much speculation about how it would turn out. Birthday cakes weren't something the Mwurandan people went in for but Matt had found a recipe online and printed it out. Amazingly, Matt had also managed to source the ingredients and everyone was looking forward to a taste of home, everyone apart from her. Although she had tried to make her excuses, the others had insisted that she must be there and in the end she had given in. After all, she didn't have to talk to Jude if she didn't want to.

Her heart gave a little lurch as it had kept on

doing whenever Jude's name had cropped up. They hadn't spoken again after they had left Bebe's room, not even to discuss their small patient's progress. Jude had made the decision to operate on the child and had drafted in Kelly to assist him, with Matt acting as his anaesthetist. When Claire had heard that, she had decided not to stay at the hospital. She'd been far too tired to be of much use anyway, so she had returned to the college with the rest of the night staff. However, from what she had heard, the operation had been textbook perfect and Bebe was expected to make a full recovery. Jude hadn't needed her help, which must have been a relief for him. He must be as eager as she was to keep his distance after what had happened that morning.

Her heart gave another jolt as she recalled how close he had come to kissing her. The worst thing was that she knew she wouldn't have stopped him if he had. She would have let him kiss her—even kissed him back!—and she couldn't help feeling guilty. Should she tell him the truth and admit that she wasn't a nun? she wondered for the hundredth time. It might make him feel better but if she did that then she would have to explain why she had misled him. Was she really prepared to do that? To lay herself open to even more heart-ache? The old fears raced round and round inside her head, making it impossible to decide. Maybe it would be better to ignore what had happened and hope that Jude would do the same.

Claire's heart was heavy as she made her way downstairs. Lesley had lent her the dress she had worn a few nights earlier as all the women had decided to dress up in Bill's honour. Bill himself looked positively resplendent in a crisp white shirt and a tie, a world away from his usual slightly scruffy self.

'I must say that you're looking very smart to-night, Dr Arnold,' Claire declared, kissing him on the cheek. She summoned a smile, not want-ing anyone to suspect how downhearted she felt. 'Having a birthday definitely suits you.'

'Hmm, I don't know about that,' Bill grumbled, tugging at his tie. 'I feel more like the Christmas turkey—all trussed up and ready for roasting!'

Claire laughed. She moved aside when someone came to join them, her laughter fading when she discovered it was Jude. He, too, had dressed up for the occasion and her breath caught as she took stock of the pale blue shirt he was wearing, a colour which provided the perfect foil for his midnight-dark hair. It took her all her time to drag her eyes away but she had to stop staring at him. It wouldn't be fair to let him see how much he affected her after what had happened that morning. It was a relief when Lesley clapped her hands and called for order.

'OK, guys. I think it's time we drank a toast to our guest of honour.' Lesley raised her glass aloft. 'To Bill. Happy birthday. Here's to the last sixty-five years and to many more to come!'

Everyone raised their glasses, apart from Claire, who hadn't picked one up. She jumped when a glass suddenly appeared in front of her.

'Here. Have mine.'

Jude pressed his glass into her hand and she automatically took a sip of the liquid, sneezing when the bubbles fizzed up her nose. Jude took the glass back off her and handed her his hand-kerchief instead, a look of mingled amusement and apology in his eyes.

'Sorry. I should have warned you it was champagne, or something masquerading as champagne rather.'

'No, no. It's fine. Really.' Claire sneezed again and hurriedly apologised. 'Sorry. This always happens if I drink sparkling wine.'

'Something to remember for future reference,' Jude replied with a smile that disappeared abruptly when he realised the significance of that comment.

Claire gave him a tight little smile and turned away. Jude sighed as he watched her walk over to Lesley and the other nurses. It was obvious that she felt uncomfortable around him and who could blame her? Would it help if he apologised again? he wondered. He had never been in this position before and he had no idea what he should do. He could end up by making matters worse and that was the last thing he wanted. Maybe it would be better to say nothing than say the wrong thing.

The evening wore on. Everyone was in very high spirits and Jude did his best to join in with the jokes and the laughter, but he was very aware that it was merely a front. Inside, in those secret places he had discovered only recently, he wasn't laughing or joking. He wasn't really sure what was happening in there except that he felt sort of flat and empty, as though he had lost something vital, something he had no hope of recovering. When Moses brought in the cake and everyone cheered, he was hard-pressed to dredge up a smile. Was this how he would continue to feel or would he get back to normal once he returned to England? His gaze went to Claire and his heart sank because he already knew the answer to that question. His life would never be the same now that he had met her.

'I don't know what to say...' There were tears in Bill's eyes as he stared at the cake. True, the icing was a rather lurid shade of green and the top layer had a decided list to starboard, but for a first attempt it was a remarkably good effort. Bill stood up and pumped Moses' hand. 'First-rate job, Moses. I really can't thank you enough for all your hard work. It's brilliant!'

Moses looked thrilled when everyone applauded him. He hurried back to the kitchen as Bill set about slicing the cake. Jude accepted a slice although the last thing he felt like was eating cake. He bit into the sponge and gagged at the overpowering taste of salt that filled his mouth. Everyone was in the same boat, all coughing and spluttering as they spat it out. Lesley wiped her mouth with a tissue and shuddered.

'Oh, yuck! I don't know what happened but something definitely went wrong. It's horrendous!'

'Yuck is right.' Amy grimaced as she pushed her plate away and turned to Matt. 'Are you sure you printed out the right recipe?'

'I think so. I mean it said all the usual things, flour, sugar, butter, eggs.' Matt looked decidedly put out at being blamed. 'I'm no cook but that's what usually goes into a cake, isn't it?'

'Maybe there was a mix-up in the kitchen,' Bill said soothingly. 'Not to worry, hey? It's the thought that counts and I really appreciate the effort you've all gone to tonight. The main thing now is to make sure that Moses doesn't find out that his masterpiece was a disaster. We don't want to hurt his feelings, do we?'

They all agreed that it was the last thing they wanted. Jude helped clear away the plates, scraping the uneaten cake into a paper bag that Kelly produced. The rest of the cake was carried upstairs to be disposed of discreetly the following morning at the hospital. Within a very short time the dining room was clear of any evidence and people were heading off to bed. Jude was the last to leave and he paused to switch off the lights.

It had been a strange night. He wasn't used to dissembling, mainly because he rarely felt so strongly about anything. He had changed so much since he had come here and he wasn't sure how he would cope when he returned home. Could he see himself going back to the work he had been doing, or would he find that he needed something more taxing that would not only stretch him but also make a real difference to people's lives?

Oh, he wasn't downplaying what he did in the private sector. Being rich wasn't a guarantee that one wouldn't experience discomfort and his patients were suitably grateful for his interventions. However, he was very aware that he hadn't pushed himself in the past few years, hadn't tried to develop his skills as he could have done. Maybe he had needed a break from the pressure of working for the NHS but it wasn't right that he continued to fritter away his talent. He didn't want to reach a point where he looked back at his life and wished he had done things differently.

It was a moment of revelation and it shook him. Jude switched off the lights, plunging the room into darkness. He glanced round when he heard footsteps on the stairs but he couldn't see who it was. It wasn't until she stepped down from the last step that he realised it was Claire.

Jude held his breath as he watched her cross the hall. He knew that he should say something to warn her he was there but he couldn't seem to speak. The words seemed to be jammed deep inside him and he couldn't push them out. She reached the door and he realised that he had to do something or risk scaring her half to death. Stepping forward, he switched on the lights again and heard her gasp.

'Sorry. I didn't mean to startle you,' he said hurriedly.

'I thought everyone had gone to bed!' she exclaimed, pressing her hand to her heart.

'I was on my way, but ended up standing here, wool-gathering,' he replied lightly. He dredged up a smile, aware that he was probably the last person Claire wanted to see. The thought was almost unbearably painful and he hurried on. 'What brought you back downstairs? After another slice of birthday cake, were you?'

'Don't!' She shuddered. 'I still can't get the taste of salt off my tongue. No, I came down to look for a button.' She held out the skirt of her dress and showed him the gap in the row of tiny pearl buttons. 'It must have fallen off and I don't want to give it back to Lesley with a button missing after she was kind enough to lend it to me.'

'Oh. I see.' Jude peered under the table, deeming it safer than standing there and admiring how she looked in the borrowed dress. His pulse gave an appreciative little leap and he crouched down so he could no longer see her. 'Ah, there it is. Under that chair. I'll get it for you.'

Kneeling down, he quickly retrieved it. Claire smiled when he handed it to her. 'Thank you. I would have felt awful if I'd lost it.' She put it in her pocket and sighed. 'Lesley is always so kind about lending me her things. I'm going to miss her when I return to England.'

'I didn't know you were going back!' Jude exclaimed.

'My visa expires soon,' she explained. 'I'll have to leave then.'

'Can't you renew it while you're here?' he suggested, his mind racing. If she was returning to England then was it possible that he could arrange to see her again? Granted, they moved in very different circles but surely they could meet up? The thought buoyed him up even though he knew how pointless it was. After all, nothing would have changed. Claire would still be set on following a path that didn't leave any room for him.

'Unfortunately not. The Mwurandan government has tightened up the rules concerning foreign nationals. There's been trouble recently about undesirable elements getting into the country, so they've decided that nobody can apply for a visa without undergoing a rigorous check first. I'll have to return to England and contact their embassy if I want to come back here.'

'And do you?' Jude asked quietly.

'I'm not sure. Maybe it's time I went back home instead of hiding away here.'

Claire bit her lip as she realised what she had said. The comment had slipped out before she'd had time to think about it and it was obvious that it had aroused Jude's curiosity.

'What do you mean? How are you hiding away here? I thought you came here to help the people of this country,' he said, frowning.

'Of course I did!' She drummed up a laugh but it was a poor effort. It certainly did nothing to convince Jude.

'Are you sure about that?' He stared at her. 'Far be it from me to question your word, Claire, but I have to say that it doesn't exactly ring true.'

'No?' She gave a little shrug as she turned to leave. 'There's not much I can do about that, I'm afraid.'

'Oh, I disagree.' He stopped her by dint of placing his hand on her arm. Although Claire knew that she could pull away any time she chose, for some reason she couldn't move a muscle. It was as though the touch of his fingers on her skin had immobilised her. She could only stand there while he looked deep into her eyes.

'You could try telling me the truth, Claire. The real truth, I mean, not the version you've told everyone else.'

Claire's heart surged in alarm. That Jude had guessed she had been less than forthcoming with everyone came as a shock. She bit her lip, feeling fear unfurling in the pit of her stomach. She didn't want to lie to him but the thought of confessing what had brought her to Mwuranda and had kept her here was more than she could bear.

How could she tell him the truth and watch his curiosity turn to revulsion?

She pulled away, her whole body trembling. Maybe she was the innocent victim but could she really expect him to see beyond what had happened to her? She couldn't bear to know that he would always think of her in future as a woman who had been raped—nothing more.

'You make it sound as though I'm hiding some dark secret!' She laughed, doing her best to feign amusement, not the easiest thing to do when her heart was aching. The thought of how Jude might react if he found out the truth made her feel sick. She knew instinctively that his reaction would affect her far more than anyone else's. 'I hate to disappoint you but there's no mystery about it. I simply decided that working here was what I wanted to do.'

'As simple as that, was it?'

The scepticism in his voice told her that he didn't believe her but there was nothing she could do. And in a way it was true. She *had* come to Mwuranda because she had wanted the job. The reason why she had wanted it was another story, and she wasn't prepared to go into that. However, the thought that it wasn't a total lie helped to appease her conscience.

'Yes. As simple as that.' She dredged up a smile, wanting to deflect his interest away from her. 'But what about you? Why did you decide to come here? It doesn't strike me that this is your usual kind of environment.'

'It isn't. I'm way out of my comfort zone and I don't mind admitting it.' He gave a small shrug, drawing her attention to the impressive width of his shoulders.

Claire took a deep breath when she felt her pulse leap. There was no point thinking about how attractive he was. No point at all. 'So what made you apply to work for Worlds Together?' she asked, needing a distraction. 'It seems a strange thing to do in the circumstances.'

'Pride.' He gave a rueful laugh. 'Someone accused me of taking the easy option and I decided to prove they were wrong. However, I'm beginning to see that they may have had a point. Suffice to say that I plan to do something about it when I get back to England.'

'I see.' Claire was intrigued by what she had heard, so much so that she longed to ask him about his future plans, but was it wise to become even more involved in his life when she should be keeping her distance? 'Well, I hope that everything works out the way you want it to,' she said, deeming it safer to let the subject drop.

'Thank you. I intend to give it my very best shot.' He hesitated. 'About this morning, Claire, I'd hate to think that you might feel awkward around me...'

'I don't,' she said quickly, not wanting to get into a discussion. Something told her that it would be the wrong thing to do when her emotions were in such turmoil. 'You were trying to comfort me and I understand that.'

'I was.'

He didn't say anything else apart from wishing her goodnight. Claire switched off the lights after he left and made her way upstairs. She knew she should be relieved to know that Jude had merely been trying to comfort her yet she couldn't deny that her heart was aching as she got into bed. Maybe it was foolish but she couldn't help wishing that he *had* kissed her, kissed her because he had wanted her, because he had desired her; because he simply couldn't help himself!

She pulled the sheet over her head, her cheeks burning. How crazy was that?

CHAPTER TWELVE

JUDE FELT VERY on edge the following morning and he knew it was his own fault. He never placed himself in the position of being vulnerable by revealing his feelings, yet he had done so with Claire. He had told her things he wouldn't have dreamt of telling anyone else and he regretted it. He needed to get back on track, shove all these thoughts and feelings back in their box and close the lid. He'd already come far too close to making a terrible mistake by nearly kissing Claire and he couldn't allow that to happen again.

It was all very unsettling. In the end, he decided to skip breakfast as he really couldn't face seeing Claire again. Matt had made good on his promise to get him some coffee and had even found him a battered old kettle as well, so at least he was able to brew himself a mug of that. He drank it standing by the bedroom window. It was another misty morning, the sun floating in a sea of red and orange as it rose above the horizon. Jude had never had much time for nature; he preferred man-made wonders, if he was honest. However, the sheer beauty of the scene unfolding before him brought a lump to his throat. Nature at her most beautiful was truly awe-inspiring.

He turned away from the view, downing the rest of the coffee in a single gulp. The sudden upsurge of emotion was yet another indication of how much he had changed and he didn't need any more reminders, thank you very much. He made his way downstairs and sat on the front steps to await the arrival of the truck, nodding as one by one the rest of the team joined him. Claire and Lesley were last to appear, Lesley giggling as she balanced a large cardboard box on her hip.

'It's the cake,' she mouthed when she saw Jude looking, and he smiled and nodded then realised with another little shock that he enjoyed being part of the conspiracy. He wouldn't have given a tinker's curse in the past but now he was as keen as everyone else to spare Moses' feelings. Was he completely changed and was it permanent? Or would he slip back into his old ways when he returned home to England?

His gaze went to Claire and he knew with a certainty that shook him that he wouldn't go back to the way he had been, that he, Jude Tobias Slater, was and always would be a very different person because of meeting her.

Claire hadn't been rostered to work in the clinic that day but when Kelly suddenly complained she was feeling sick, she immediately offered to swap places with her. While Kelly rushed off to the bathroom, Claire gathered together the notes for the dozen or so repeat appointments who would be seen first. Ten-year-old Jeremiah was the first on the list and he came hurrying over when she went to collect him from the waiting room.

'So how are you today, Jeremiah?' she asked, holding his hand as she led him to the screened-off area in the corner. She knew that Jude was duty doctor that day and steeled herself before pushing back the screen. No way was she going to react when she saw him, she told herself sternly. She was going to treat him the same as everyone else—politely and professionally. After last night, she would be mad to do anything else.

'I'm good, Sister Claire,' Jeremiah replied, his face breaking into a huge grin when he saw Jude sitting behind the makeshift desk. Letting go of her hand, he hurried straight over to him. 'Did you see the pictures of my bones, Mr Doctor, and can you make my leg better?'

'That's what we need to talk about.'

Jude stood up and came around the table. He barely glanced at Claire as he bent to look at the little boy and for some perverse reason she took exception to his lack of attention. Did he have to make it quite so clear how easy it was to ignore her?

'I've had a really good look at the pictures, Jeremiah, and I'm very sorry to say that there isn't anything I can do that will make your leg any better.'

Claire set aside her own feelings when she

heard what Jude had said. Hurrying forward, she put her arm around Jeremiah's shoulders when he started to cry. She knew how devastated he must feel as he had been hoping that something could be done so that he would be able to play football—his passion—with the other boys.

'Don't cry, sweetheart. Maybe you can practise being goalkeeper. That way you won't have to run around as much, will you? What do you think, Dr Slater?'

'It's an idea,' Jude replied, although she heard the doubt in his voice. It was obvious that Jeremiah had heard it too because he pulled away from her.

'No! I can't be goalkeeper. I can't be anything with this stupid leg!'

He spun round and hurried out of the cubicle. Claire ran after him, quickly explaining what had happened to Sister Anne. She bit her lip as she watched the elderly nun lead him away. It seemed so unfair that nothing could be done to help a child like Jeremiah, who had been through so much in his short life. Her heart was heavy as she made her way back to the cubicle. Jude was seated behind the table again and he looked up when she went in.

'Is he OK?'

'Not really. I think he was pinning his hopes on you being able to do something.'

'I wish I could, but the fact is that I simply don't have the expertise to undertake such a complex operation.'

He sighed as he ran his hands through his hair. Claire felt a ripple of sympathy run through her when she realised how upset he looked. Being the bearer of such unwelcome news had taken its toll on him.

'It isn't your fault, Jude,' she said softly.

'No? Then whose fault is it? I'm a surgeon and I'm supposed to help people. Maybe if I hadn't wasted so many years then I might have been able to give that poor kid a better future to look forward to. But, no, instead of developing my skills, I've spent my time performing minor operations!'

Claire could hear the frustration in his voice.

Jude may have had his own reasons for coming to Mwuranda but he genuinely wanted to help the people here. It made her wonder all of a sudden if he would feel the same about her if she told him what had happened, that she had been raped.

The thought was far too tempting. It was a relief when he asked her to call in their next patient. They worked their way through the repeat appointments then started on the newcomers. There were dozens of them as usual, so they were kept busy for the rest of the afternoon, but Claire was glad. It was better to be busy than allow herself to explore that dangerously tempting idea. Once she told Jude there would be no going back; she would have to face whatever happened. She sighed. She wasn't sure if she was ready for that.

The day drew to a close but Jude was too restless to sleep. Claire had returned to the convent, so it wasn't her presence that was unsettling him. It was the thought of Jeremiah and how devastated the boy had been that was causing the problem. He had brought the X-rays back with him and he spread them on the dining room table after everyone had gone upstairs. There were half a dozen in total and he held them up to the light in turn. The boy's leg had been broken in several places and that was why it would be such a complex operation to repair it. Quite apart from his lack of expertise in this field, they simply didn't have the facilities here to undertake this kind of surgery. However, if Jeremiah could be treated in the UK then it might be a different story; there was a strong chance that his leg could be repaired or, at least, improved.

A rush of renewed optimism filled him as he gathered up the films and took them upstairs. He hadn't used his laptop since he had arrived and the battery was flat but he plugged it in, praying that they wouldn't have a power cut. Maybe he couldn't perform the surgery Jeremiah needed but he knew someone who could—if he would agree. And if he could obtain permission to take Jeremiah *out* of Mwuranda and *into* England.

Jude took a deep breath and made himself stop right there. He would take it one step at a time, face any problems as and when they arose. Just for a moment he found himself wondering what Claire would think if he managed to set everything in motion before he drove the thought from his head. He wasn't doing this to improve her opinion of him. He was doing it for the sake of a ten-year-old boy who had been dealt a rotten hand. However, one thing was certain: he would never find himself in the position of being unable to help again!

Claire managed to get a lift to the hospital on the supply truck the following morning, so she arrived well before the others. Jeremiah had been inconsolable all the previous evening and she only hoped that the sisters could find a way to alleviate his disappointment, although it seemed unlikely that anything would help. She was feeling more than a little downhearted as she went into the office to sign in, only to stop in surprise when she found Jude bent over the computer.

'I didn't realise everyone had arrived,' she said in surprise.

'They haven't. I came on ahead on the bike as I wanted to email these to London.' He held up a wedge of X-rays and Claire frowned.

'Aren't they Jeremiah's?'

'Uh-huh.' Jude made a final check then pressed the send key. 'I'm emailing them to Professor Jackson, my old tutor. He's agreed to take a look at them and see if there's anything he can do for Jeremiah.'

'Really? Oh, that's wonderful!' Claire exclaimed.

'We'd better not count our chickens just yet,' he warned her. 'That leg is a mess and there's no guarantee that even the Professor will be able to do anything with it.'

'But you must think there's a chance he can or you wouldn't have contacted him,' she pointed out.

'Yes. If anyone can help Jeremiah, it's him. He's a brilliant surgeon—there's no other way to describe him. Some of the work he's done is staggering.'

'A bit of a hero of yours, I take it?' Claire said with a smile.

'I suppose so.' Jude frowned. 'I've never really thought about it but you're right. The Professor is definitely someone I look up to, even though he gave me a very hard time when I last saw him.'

'Really? Why was that?' she asked curiously.

'Oh, because he didn't think I was making full use of my training.' He sighed. 'It was the Professor who accused me of taking the easy option. The worst thing is that I agree with him. I might have been able to help Jeremiah myself if I'd not opted to work in the private sector for all this time.'

'I doubt if you've had such an easy ride,' Claire countered, hating to hear him berate himself. From what she had seen there was no question that Jude was a first-rate surgeon. 'I know how hard you must have had to work to qualify as a surgeon—it's one of the most exacting areas of medicine. The hours alone are crippling.'

'True.' He grinned. 'You're very good for my ego, Claire. Do you know that?'

Claire felt a little rush of pleasure and smiled at him. 'I'm only telling the truth.'

'Well, thank you anyway. I don't feel half as guilty now for not being able to do anything for Jeremiah.' His eyes met hers, dark and deep and filled with something that made a shiver run through her. When he took a step towards her, she didn't move, held by the intensity of his gaze...

'Hello! What's going on in here?'

Lola bustled into the office and the moment passed. Claire took a quick breath, struggling to pull herself together. However, she knew that if they hadn't been interrupted then she would have been in Jude's arms right now.

'I came in early to use your computer. I hope you don't mind.'

There was a roughness to Jude's voice that told her he was finding it as difficult as she was to behave normally. Claire shot a wary glance at him and felt her heart lurch when she saw how strained he looked. It was clear from his expression that he knew what would have happened if they hadn't been interrupted and it didn't make sense. He had explained that near-miss kiss by claiming he had been trying to comfort her and she had believed him. However, it didn't explain what had happened just now. As she filled in the sheet, she found herself wondering how far it would have gone if they'd been somewhere private. Would the desire to be held have progressed to something more?

Claire shuddered as she realised how easily it could have done. But how would she cope with intimacy after what had happened to her? Would it be the life-affirming experience it should be or a horrendous ordeal? There was no way of knowing until she took that final step and she wasn't sure if she could do that.

She glanced over at Jude, who was showing Lola the X-rays. Although she knew in her heart that he would never willingly hurt her, was it enough to overcome her fear and help her find the courage she needed?

Jude managed to hold on to his composure but it was a close call. Javid was coming along the corridor when he left the office and he made some joking remark about Jude earning himself extra brownie points for his early start. Jude responded and he must have made sense too because Javid laughed, but he had no idea what he had said. His mind was too full of what had happened. Claire had been about to step into his arms—he knew she had! And once she'd been in them then who knew where it would have led? Hell's bells! That was enough to boggle any man's mind!

He about-turned and headed outside, needing some air. The sun had risen now and the temperature was mounting but he wasn't aware of the heat as he made his way to the pool. Although he had been invited to join the others for a swim on several occasions, he hadn't been back there. For some reason the thought of cooling off in the deep green water hadn't held any appeal. Now, as he gazed across the water, he understood why. He hadn't felt tempted to return because Claire wouldn't have been there. It was being with her that had made it so special.

Jude closed his eyes and let his mind wander,

unsurprised when it started to conjure up a whole series of images. And every single one of them involved Claire: his first glimpse of her in that hideous old boiler suit; how slender her body had felt when he had put his arms around her yesterday; the look on her face as he had taken that single step towards her...

Jude opened his eyes and stared at the water. He needed to ask himself a question and it was such a momentous one that he needed every faculty in full working order. Was he falling in love with Claire or was it the fact that he was so far removed from everything he knew that he was misinterpreting his feelings?

He stood there for a long time, waiting for the answer to come to him, but it remained stubbornly out of reach. He sighed as he turned around and made his way back to the hospital. He would have to wait a while longer, it appeared, and in the meantime he would do what he'd said he would and stay away from Claire. Falling in love had never been on his agenda, and falling in love with a woman who could never love him in return would be a huge mistake. If there was any way to stop it happening then he would find it, so help him!

CHAPTER THIRTEEN

THE TIME FLEW PAST, one day running into the next without a pause. They didn't even stop at the weekends but worked straight through. It was a gruelling schedule which was why most people only remained in Mwuranda for three months at a time. Claire was the exception, although she knew that she would have to leave soon. She wasn't surprised, therefore, when a letter arrived, informing her that she must leave the country in two weeks' time when her visa expired.

She showed the letter to Lesley as they rode into town on the truck. She had stayed over at the college the night before as there had been no transport available to ferry her back to the convent. She had tried to avoid staying there since that morning in the office. The memory of what had so nearly happened between her and Jude was still very raw and it had seemed wiser to keep out of his way. However, she'd had no choice other than to stay, but as Jude had been rostered for the night shift, it had made it easier.

'So that's it, then. You must be looking forward to going back to England, Claire, even if it's only for a rest.' Lesley grimaced as she handed back the letter. 'I have to admit that I'm more than ready to go home and I've only been here for a fraction of the time you have.'

'I suppose so,' Claire replied as she slipped the letter into her pocket.

'Only suppose?' Lesley frowned. 'Aren't you looking forward to seeing your family and friends again?'

'Yes, of course I am.' Claire dredged up a smile, although the thought of being back in London was making her feel rather anxious. She still wasn't sure how she would cope if she saw Andrew again.

'Hmm. Well, I have to say that it doesn't sound like it,' Lesley retorted. 'Could it be the thought of leaving behind the handsome Dr Slater that's taking the shine off the idea?'

'No! Don't be ridiculous!' Claire exclaimed. She felt the colour run up her face when Lesley treated her to an old-fashioned look. 'Jude has nothing to do with it—that's the truth.'

'Methinks the lady doth protest too much,' Lesley misquoted with a grin. 'Come on, love, you know you fancy him something rotten. It's as plain as the nose on your face, as is the fact that he feels the same about you. What I don't understand is why you're so determined to keep him at arm's length. You're young, free and single, so why not do what comes naturally?'

'You're wrong. I don't fancy him,' Claire protested, although she knew that Lesley wouldn't believe her.

Fortunately, they had reached the hospital and she was able to make her escape, but the thought plagued her for the rest of the day. Was she making a mistake by avoiding getting involved with Jude? As Lesley had pointed out, there was nothing to stop her, so why didn't she come clean, admit that she wasn't a nun and have an affair with him?

Maybe it was what she needed to finally kill off the demons from her past. If she could prove to herself that she could cope with intimacy then what had happened would no longer rule her life. She didn't *have* to tell Jude about the rape either. It could remain her secret. There was no law that said you had to tell someone every little detail about your life, was there?

Her thoughts whirled as though they were on a merry-go-round but she still couldn't make up her mind what to do. The thought of withholding the truth from him if they did start a relationship didn't sit easily with her and yet the alternative was equally unpalatable. If she knew how he would react if she told him, it would be easier to decide, but that was something she couldn't foretell. She couldn't bear it if he looked at her with disgust once he found out. It would break her heart.

* * *

Jude only found out that Claire was leaving by chance when he overheard Lesley and Amy talking at dinner that night. He bent over his plate, struggling to get a grip as his emotions ran riot. He knew that Claire had been avoiding him since that morning in the office but he couldn't complain as he had been avoiding her too. Despite trying to pin down his feelings, he still wasn't sure how he felt. Oh, he was attracted to her—there was no question about that. He wanted her more than he had wanted any woman and not just physically either. He wanted to spend time with her—talking, laughing or even sitting in silence—and he had never felt that way about anyone before. But was it love? Real love? The kind that lasted for ever and ever?

The nagging thought that his feelings were intensified by the fact he was so far removed from his natural habitat lingered at the back of his mind and he was afraid of making a mistake, especially when it wouldn't make a scrap of difference to the outcome. He couldn't have Claire and even if he *was* falling in love with her, nothing would change in that respect, so why torture himself by wishing for the impossible? By the time he went to his room after dinner had finished, Jude's spirits were at an all-time low. He had come to Mwuranda to prove himself. What he had never expected was that it would turn his whole world upside down.

Claire had taken the morning off to pack. There was a plane due the following day bringing in fresh supplies and the plan was that she would fly back to England on it. Although there was another week left on her visa, it would only complicate matters if she booked herself onto a scheduled flight. Flights in and out of Mwuranda were dicey at the best of times and could be cancelled without warning. She didn't want to risk falling foul of the authorities by outstaying her visa. She had just finished packing the few clothes she planned to take back with her when one of the nuns came hurrying into the room and asked her if she had seen Jeremiah. Apparently, he hadn't turned up for lessons and no one had seen him since breakfast.

Claire abandoned her packing while she helped the sisters search the convent but there was no sign of him inside or out. He had become increasingly withdrawn since he had been told that nothing could be done about his leg and several times had gone off on his own. However, he had never been missing for this long. While Sister Julie went inside to telephone the hospital in case he had found his way there, Claire decided to check the route he would have taken. She was worried in case he had fallen and injured himself and was unable to get back.

The air was stifling as she left the convent. She was wearing one of the nuns' dresses again that day and she could feel the sun burning through the light grey cotton. It was only a few miles to the hospital, although the nuns never walked there. There were still rebel factions operating in the area and it was safer to be driven there and back. Claire kept a wary eye on the surrounding scrubland as she followed the path, but she saw no sign of the rebels. She also saw no sign of Jeremiah and her concern intensified as she reached the trees that marked the boundary of the hospital's grounds. Where on earth had he got to?

She went to step out of the trees then stopped abruptly when the sound of gunfire ripped across the clearing. Dropping to the ground, she tried to make out where it was coming from, her heart sinking when she spotted a group of men at the opposite side of the clearing. They were obviously rebel soldiers although she had no idea why they had decided to attack the hospital. The Worlds Together team had made it clear that they were impartial. It meant that they had been able to carry out their work in relative safety. What had happened to change that was a mystery, but there was little doubt that the hospital was under attack.

Claire remained where she was while she debated her options. She was just trying to decide if the nun's habit would offer her any protection when a movement caught her eye. Alarm ran through her when she spotted Jeremiah standing amongst the trees. It was obvious that he was about to make a run for it to reach the hospital and that was the last thing he must do. The rebels offered no concessions when it came to age; they would gun down a child as readily as they would a grown man. Claire knew she had to stop him and that to do so she had to put herself at risk. Stepping out of the trees, she shouted to him.

'Stay there! Do you hear me, Jeremiah? Don't move!'

There was another volley of shots and she gasped when she felt a burning pain in her right thigh. She fell to the ground, holding her breath when she realised that Jeremiah had ignored her and was attempting to cross the clearing. A man suddenly ran out of the hospital and her heart leapt when she recognised Jude. He picked up Jeremiah and carried him to safety then turned around and headed straight to her.

Claire watched in horror, sure that he would get himself shot, but, miraculously, he made it safely. He dropped to his knees beside her and her breath caught when she saw the expression on his face. She had never seen such fear on anyone's face before, but why? Because he feared for his own life, or because he was afraid for her? She had no idea, but the thought that he might care so much about her filled her with joy. In that second she finally admitted what she had been trying to deny for weeks: she wanted Jude to care about her. She wanted him to love her.

'Is it just your leg that's been hit?' Jude demanded, clamping down on the fear that was turning his blood to ice. He couldn't afford to fall apart. Claire needed him to be strong and he mustn't let her down. 'Claire, listen to me!' he instructed urgently when she failed to answer. 'Have you been hit anywhere else apart from your leg?'

Even before she could answer the question, his hands began moving over her. Although her leg was bleeding copiously, he could tell from the flow that the bullet hadn't hit an artery. If that had happened then she could have bled to death right here in front of him. His hands shook at the thought.

'No. It's just my leg that's been hit.' She lifted her skirt and showed him the wound, shuddering at the sight of her torn flesh.

'Here, let me see.' Jude bent over so she couldn't see how terrified he felt. The thought of losing her was unbearable. 'Well, I'm no expert. The patients I normally treat don't go around getting themselves shot. However, from what little knowledge I do have, I'd say it's a flesh wound. Once we've stopped the bleeding, it shouldn't be too difficult to treat it.'

He tore a strip of cloth off the bottom of his shirt and balled it up then pressed it against the wound. He grimaced when she winced. 'Sorry. I know it must hurt like blazes but I need to put pressure on it to stop the bleeding.'

'It's all right,' she muttered, dashing away the tears that had sprung to her eyes. She gave a wobbly little laugh that tugged at his heartstrings. 'Take no notice—I'm just being a baby.'

'Of course you aren't,' Jude countered roughly. Reaching out, he pulled her into his arms, uncaring if it was the wrong thing to do. She was in pain and no matter if she was a nun, she was a human being and needed comforting.

He drew her to him, feeling a rush of emotions hit him. Her body felt so small and slender as she nestled against him, the soft curves of her breasts pushing against his chest, and he was overwhelmed by tenderness. He wanted to hold her like this for ever, to keep her safe in his arms and protect her from harm for the rest of his days. Was this how love made you feel? he wondered giddily. Did it make you put the other person's needs before your own, make you worry about *their* safety and *their* happiness at the expense of your own?

Jude knew it was true and the realisation filled him with both euphoria and despair. He loved Claire and he needed to face up to how he felt, face up to the fact that his love would never be reciprocated either. Claire would never love him in return and the thought was so raw and so painful that it spurred him on to do what he had sworn he would never do. Bending, he took her mouth in a kiss that was compounded of everything he was feeling, from the heights of joy to the depths of despair. It was a kiss that he knew should never have happened. It was a kiss he needed.

CHAPTER FOURTEEN

CLAIRE FELT DESIRE rush through her as Jude's mouth closed over hers. In that moment she realised how much she had been longing for this to happen. In some inexplicable way she had sensed that it would change her, make her feel differently, and it did. She felt like *her* when Jude kissed her, like the woman she had been who had enjoyed life and hadn't been afraid. It was such a wonderful feeling that she kissed him back, wanting him to know how much he meant to her...

The sound of gunfire brought them back to earth with a thud. Claire gasped when Jude pushed her away. His face was set as he stood up and stared across the clearing, and the first little doubt came trickling back. Did he regret what he had done, wish that he hadn't broken his promise? She bit her lip as the question was followed by another: had Jude kissed her not because of who she was but because it had been an instinctive response to holding a woman in his arms?

'We need to get back to the hospital. The rebels are starting to move and we won't stand a chance if they find us.' His voice was clipped although whether it was the precariousness of their situation that was causing it or what had happened, she wasn't sure.

'What do you suggest?' she asked, trying to keep the pain out of her voice. It wasn't his fault if he had acted out of instinct and she mustn't blame him.

'We need some kind of a diversion. If we can distract them then there's a chance we can get to the hospital.' He glanced at her leg which, thankfully, had stopped bleeding now. 'If I bind up your leg do you think you can walk on it?'

'I'll try.' She watched him tear another strip off his shirt. He bound it tightly around her thigh then helped her up. Claire gasped when a sear-ing pain shot through her leg as soon as she put her weight on it.

Jude shook his head. 'You're not going to be able to get far on that leg. I'll have to carry you, so we definitely need to set up some kind of a diversion first.'

He helped her sit down again then went to the edge of the trees. Claire could see someone standing at one of the upper windows and realised it was Matt Kearney. Jude had seen him too and started signalling to him, and after a couple of minutes Matt gave him the thumbs-up sign and disappeared.

'Let's hope Matt manages to find something really good to distract them,' Jude said grimly as he helped her to her feet once more. He swung her up into his arms, his expression never altering as he settled her against his chest. He appeared so completely detached that Claire realised her suspicions had been correct. Jude may have kissed her but he would have done the same to any woman in the circumstances.

Thankfully, she had no time to dwell on that

thought before there was a series of loud explosions from the rear of the hospital. She gasped when she saw dozens of rockets shooting skywards. More fireworks went off, sending out showers of brightly coloured sparks, but Jude didn't stop to watch them. He ran out from the trees, weaving from side to side so they wouldn't present such an easy target, but in the event not a single shot was fired at them. Willing hands reached out and pulled them inside when they reached the hospital.

'Put her on this trolley.'

Bill rapped out instructions in a wholly unfamiliar fashion and moments later Claire found herself being rushed to Theatre. Javid was already there, all scrubbed up and waiting. While Bill started the anaesthetic, she found herself wondering why Jude wasn't performing the operation. He was the lead surgeon, after all, but maybe he didn't consider her injuries serious enough to require his attention. Just because he had kissed her, it didn't mean that he thought she was special. The thought accompanied her as she slid into unconsciousness, a dark cloud at the back of her mind.

Jude paced the office, unable to sit still while he waited for news of Claire. The operation seemed to be taking an inordinate amount of time and it made him wonder if Javid had hit a snag. Even though he had agreed with Bill that it would be better if someone else performed the surgery, maybe he should go and check, he decided, flinging open the door...

And maybe he should leave well alone, an inner voice cautioned. *Hadn't he caused enough problems without creating any more?*

Jude's expression was grim as he closed the door. Walking over to the desk, he sat down while he thought about what had happened. Matt's diversion had proved highly effective. Not only had it allowed him and Claire to reach the safety of the hospital but it had brought the government troops racing to their aid. The rebel fighters had all been captured which meant they were safe for now. Apparently, a rumour had been going round that one of the highest-ranking generals in charge of the military had been admitted to the hospital which was why they had come under attack. Jude wasn't sure how it had started but it had caused a major disruption. And not only to the smooth running of the hospital either.

He put his head in his hands and groaned. To say that he regretted kissing Claire was a massive understatement. Not only had he made a fool of himself but he must have embarrassed her as well. How he was going to explain himself when he saw her, he had no idea. He couldn't tell her the truth; that he had fallen in love with her and wanted to spend the rest of his days with her!

'Ah, so here you are.' Javid suddenly appeared and Jude jumped up.

'How did it go?' he rapped out, unable to contain his anxiety. 'Was there a problem? It seemed to take an awfully long time.'

'Did it?' Javid glanced at the clock over the desk and shrugged. 'It didn't seem that long to me...' He broke off when Jude glared at him. 'Anyway, Claire's fine. It was just a flesh wound—the bullet must have clipped her thigh as it passed. I cleaned everything up, got rid of a few fibres from her dress that were lodged in the wound, and that was it, basically.'

'So she'll be fit enough to fly back to England tomorrow,' Jude said quietly, struggling to get a grip. He certainly didn't want to compound his errors by making Javid think that he doubted his ability.

'Oh, yes. Her leg will be painful for a week or so but it shouldn't cause any lasting damage, I'm pleased to say. No, she was incredibly lucky, all things considered.'

'She was,' Jude agreed. He thanked Javid then took a deep breath before following him from the room. He wasn't looking forward to the next few minutes but he owed Claire an apology and he needed to do it now because he wouldn't get another chance with her leaving in the morning. All he could hope was that he would be able to come up with something to explain his actions, something that wouldn't necessitate him telling her the truth. One thing was certain: Claire wouldn't welcome it if he told her that he loved her.

The effects of the anaesthetic had worn off fairly quickly. Although her head still felt a little muzzy, otherwise Claire felt fine. Bill had insisted on staying with her but now she chivvied him to take a break. It was the middle of the afternoon and, with one thing and another, lunch had been a non-starter.

She closed her eyes after Bill left. Whether it was the after-effects of the anaesthetic, the events of the day had taken on a surreal quality. She found it difficult to believe that she had been shot yet she had the dressing on her thigh to prove it. Her thoughts drifted on, inevitably coming back to that kiss. Had it been *her* Jude had wanted to kiss with such passion or would any woman have done?

The door opened as someone came into the room but it was a moment before Claire opened her eyes. She fixed a smile to her mouth as she turned to greet her visitor, not wanting anyone to suspect how much the idea hurt. It came as a huge shock to find Jude himself standing at the end of her bed.

'So how do you feel? Javid said everything went swimmingly,' he said coolly.

'I'm fine.' She gave a little shrug, determined to match his tone. She certainly wouldn't embarrass herself by letting him know how painful she found it to be treated so coldly. 'My head's a bit woozy from the anaesthetic but that's all.'

'Good.' Picking up the chart from the end of the bed, he skimmed through it. He hung it back in place and Claire felt a ripple run through her when she saw that his hands were shaking. Maybe he wasn't as indifferent as he was pretending, she thought. The idea made her head spin so that she missed what he said. It was only when she realised that he was waiting for her to speak that she pulled herself together.

'I'm sorry—what did you say?'

'I said that I owe you an apology, and I do. I should never have kissed you, Claire. Put it down to the heat of the moment, although that's no excuse. However, I want you to know that I bitterly regret my actions.'

Claire didn't have time to say anything before he swung round and left the room. But then what could she have said? she thought despairingly. That he hadn't embarrassed her, that on the contrary she had welcomed his kiss and wanted him to kiss her again? An admission like that was bound to have led to questions and she still wasn't ready to answer them and explain about her past.

Tears began to pour down her face. It was better to leave things the way they were, to leave Jude still believing that she was someone she wasn't: a pure and innocent woman.

Jude had never felt more wretched in his entire life. He lay awake all night thinking about what had happened. Far from making him feel better, apologising to Claire had made him feel worse. He knew that he had been far too economical with the truth but what else could he have said? Surely it was better if she believed he was some kind of...*serial kisser* than embarrass her even more by admitting that he loved her!

Lesley was in the dining room when he went down for breakfast. She took one look at him and rolled her eyes. 'No need to ask how you slept,' she said wryly. 'You look dreadful!'

'I'm fine,' Jude stated huffily. He went to the buffet but the sight of food made his stomach churn. The plane was due to leave in an hour's time and every second that ticked past brought the moment when Claire would go out of his life for good that bit closer. That he would never see her again was guaranteed. She wouldn't contact him and he certainly couldn't contact her now. No, this was it, the not-so-grand finale, the end of any foolish dreams he had harboured...

'For heaven's sake, man, do something!' Lesley stood up and came over to him. 'You can't just let her go. It's obvious that you're crazy about her, so go and tell her that instead of mooning about here like some lost soul!'

'What's the point?' He couldn't even drum up any anger, although if anyone had spoken to him in that fashion in the past he would have had their guts for the proverbial garters. 'Claire isn't interested in how I feel. Her future is all mapped out and there isn't any place in it for me.'

'The *point* is that things aren't always what they appear to be,' Lesley shot back, glaring at him. 'I can't say anything more—it's up to Claire. But believe me when I say that you're making a huge mistake by letting her leave like this.'

Lesley stalked out of the room. Jude went to follow her and demand to know what she'd meant then suddenly thought better of it. It was obvious that Lesley had said everything she intended to say and now it was up to him what happened. The question he needed to ask himself was whether he was willing to risk making a fool of himself again.

His feet were already moving before the answer presented itself, carrying him out of the dining room and across the hall. By the time he reached the front steps he was running, racing around the building to where he had parked the motorbike. He swung his leg over the saddle, sending up a prayer that the engine would start. He didn't have time to coax it to life, not when the plane that was due to take Claire away was waiting on the runway.

The engine fired first time, rattling and coughing in protest, but working all the same. Jude set off in a shower of dust. It took forty minutes to reach the airfield which meant he had ten minutes to spare, ten minutes to change Claire's mind about the future she had planned. Was he right to attempt such a thing? He didn't know. But if he let her leave without telling her that he loved her, he would always regret it!

Claire had been ferried to the airfield in one of the trucks. Although her leg was extremely painful, she could manage to walk with the aid of crutches. Bill had insisted on waiting with her and they sat on a couple of empty packing cases while the crew ran through the pre-flight checks.

They didn't speak. Claire had nothing to say and Bill obviously recognised her desire for silence. It was as though every scrap of emotion she was capable of feeling had seeped away. In a few minutes' time she would get on that plane and she would never see Jude again.

The sound of an engine cut through the silence. Bill stood up and turned towards the road. 'What the devil's going on!' he exclaimed.

Claire glanced round, although she really didn't care what was happening. Her heart suddenly seized up when she recognised the man astride the motorbike. What was Jude doing here? Surely he had said everything yesterday? It had been the heat of the moment that had caused him to kiss her and he regretted it. What else was there to say?

She struggled to her feet, trembling all over as she watched him bring the bike to an unsteady halt. He propped it against the fence then came striding over to them. His face was set but there was something about the expression in his eyes that made her heart suddenly start beating again. If he regretted what had happened then why was he looking at her that way?

'I'll just go and check how the guys are doing.'

Bill hurriedly excused himself but Claire was barely aware of him leaving. Every fibre of her being was focused on the man in front of her. His face was pale beneath his tan, his eyes surrounded by heavy shadows. Jude hadn't slept from the look of him but why was that? Why had he lain awake all night when he had dismissed that kiss?

'I need to tell you something, Claire, although I'm not sure if you'll want to hear it.' His voice grated, filled with so many emotions that it was impossible to sort one out from another, so Claire didn't try. She simply stood there and after a moment he carried on.

'There was a reason why I kissed you yesterday and it had nothing to do with the heat of the moment either.'

He took hold of her hand and she had a feeling that he needed the contact to bolster his courage. The thought shocked her so much that the numbness which had enveloped her melted away. That this proud, self-possessed man needed her touch was humbling. It was an effort to concentrate when he continued.

'I had to kiss you, Claire—I couldn't help myself and that's the truth of the matter. I...well, I think I'm falling in love with you even though I know I shouldn't let it happen.'

Jude could feel the blood pounding through his veins. Claire hadn't said a word and her silence simply compounded his worst fears. Was she shocked by what he had said? Dismayed by such an unwelcome declaration? *Disgusted* even that he should dare to feel this way about her? He swung round, knowing that the only thing he could do was to beat a hasty retreat. He didn't want to put her under any more pressure, definitely didn't want her thinking that she had to try to spare his feelings...

'Wait!'

Jude stopped reluctantly, although he didn't turn round. He couldn't bring himself to do that in case he saw pity in her eyes. His pride may have been battered to a pulp but he had something left, so help him! 'Yes?'

'You can't tell me that and then just walk away!'

The anger in her voice brought him swinging round and he stared at her in shock because it wasn't the reaction he'd expected. 'I'm sorry,' he began. 'I know I shouldn't have said anything…'

'No, you damned well shouldn't!' She limped over to him, leaning heavily on the crutches as she glared up into his face. 'I didn't think you were a coward, Jude Slater, but that's what you are, an out-and-out coward!'

She gave him a none-too-gentle poke in the chest with one of the crutches and Jude took a step back, trying to think of something to say in his defence. However, it appeared she hadn't finished. 'You could have told me yesterday how you felt, or *any* day at all, come to that, but, no, you had to wait until I'm about to leave.'

'I'm sorry,' he began again then stopped when he realised he was repeating himself.

'And you think that's enough, do you? You honestly think that another apology is going to make everything right?'

She shook her head, her silky blonde hair swirling around her shoulders, and Jude felt his body choose that particular moment to stir itself to life. He had never seen her so angry before and, hackneyed though it sounded, he couldn't help thinking how beautiful she looked.

'I hoped it would,' he said softly, wondering if she could hear the desire in his voice.

'Well, you were mistaken!' she shot back, but he saw the colour that rose to her cheeks and knew she had heard it. The strange thing was that she didn't look shocked or disgusted either.

Jude was just trying to get his head round that idea when Bill came over to them, raising his voice to make himself heard as the plane's engines started up.

'Sorry to butt in, folks, but the pilot's ready to take off, so you'll have to get on board.'

'Oh, right.' Claire swivelled round and kissed Bill on the cheek. 'Thanks for everything, Bill,' she said, pitching her voice to carry above the roar of the engines. 'You've been a wonderful friend.'

'My pleasure, love.'

Bill gave her a fatherly hug then moved away, obviously wanting to afford them some privacy. Jude held his breath when Claire turned to him. He wanted more than a perfunctory kiss on the cheek but after what had happened just now he'd be lucky to get that. She looked him straight in the eyes then suddenly leant forward and he froze when, instead of kissing his cheek, she kissed him on the mouth. Her lips clung to his for a moment before she turned her head and whispered something in his ear.

'What did you say?' he demanded, but she was already walking towards the plane. One of the crew helped her on board and the next moment the doors closed and that was that; Jude could only stand and watch as the plane took off.

'See you later, son.'

Bill clapped him on the shoulder then headed over to the truck, but Jude stayed right where he was. Closing his eyes, he tried to make sense of what had happened. The noise from the plane's engines had made it difficult to hear properly but he could have sworn that Claire had whispered, *'I am not a nun.'*

Jude's eyes flew open and he watched until the plane disappeared from sight, those five little words ringing in his ears. Was it true or had he misheard her? He had no idea but one thing was certain: he intended to find out!

CHAPTER FIFTEEN

A MONTH PASSED and Claire gradually settled back into life in England. Her leg had healed and she no longer needed the crutches to get around. She had moved into temporary accommodation, renting a bedsit on the outskirts of London until she found herself a job. She had applied for three nursing posts and was waiting to be interviewed.

On the surface her life was running smoothly but underneath the apparent order was a lot of uncertainty. Would Jude get in touch with her when he returned to England or would he decide that he wanted nothing more to do with her? After all, she had deliberately misled him, so who could blame him if he chose not to see her again? Then there was the question of how she felt about seeing him when it would mean her having to tell him the rest of the story. The fear of how he might react hadn't gone away; if anything it had grown stronger because she had so much more to lose. She couldn't bear it if his love turned to revulsion once he found out what had happened to her.

It was all very unsettling. Claire found herself going over and over it day after day. Lesley had given Claire her mobile phone number with strict instructions to text her with her new address, but she thought long and hard before doing so. Although it was tempting to simply disappear, she knew it would be wrong to take the easy way out. Apart from the fact that she wanted to stay in touch with Lesley, it wouldn't be fair to Jude. She had accused him of being a coward and she couldn't behave in the same way. The team was due to return at the end of the following month, not that there was any guarantee he would want to see her. Once he was back on home ground his feelings could change. She wasn't sure if that idea made her feel better or worse. When her doorbell rang late one Friday night, she assumed it was a visitor for one of the other tenants ringing it by mistake. It came as a massive shock when she heard Jude's voice coming over the entry-phone speaker.

'Claire, it's me, Jude. Can you let me in, please?'

Claire's heart began to pound as she pressed the button to unlock the main doors. She had no idea why he had returned early but that was less important than why he had come to see her at this hour. It was almost midnight and far too late for a social call. Whatever had brought him here had to be extremely urgent.

Jude could feel the tension that had gripped him for the past twenty-four hours reach a crescendo. He knew that he should have left it until the morning before he saw Claire but he couldn't stand the strain any longer. He had spent the past month thinking about what she had said and now he needed answers. What it all boiled down to was why had she let him believe that she was a nun?

His heart was racing when he reached the first floor. Claire was standing by the door and he sighed when he saw how strained she looked. Did she regret telling him the truth, wish that she hadn't said anything? He had no idea but the tiny ray of hope that it had been an encouraging sign flickered even if it didn't quite disappear.

'Come in.'

She led him inside, closing the door behind them. Jude took a long look around although there wasn't much to see. The whole place could have fitted into one room of his apartment and he felt a rush of anger at the thought. Claire deserved better than this shabby little room!

'I didn't think you were due back yet.' She sat down on the sofa which obviously doubled as her bed and Jude pulled himself together. He hadn't come here to dis her living arrangements.

'We weren't.' He opted for the single chair and sat down. 'Unfortunately, there's been a lot of unrest recently and it was deemed too dangerous for us to stay out there.'

'I see.' Claire frowned. 'I'm surprised Lesley didn't text to tell me.'

'I asked her not to.'

'Why on earth did you do that?'

'Because I was afraid that you would take steps to avoid seeing me if you knew I was back.' Jude leant forward, feeling the tension twisting his insides into knots. 'I need to know if what you said before you left was true, Claire. Was it? Are you a nun?'

'No. I'm not.'

Her voice was low but Jude felt its effects all the same. He took a deep breath, struggling to hang on to his control. 'Then why did you let me believe that you were?'

'Because I was afraid.'

'Afraid,' he repeated because it was the last thing he had expected to hear. 'Afraid of me, do you mean?'

'Yes. I realised that you had an…effect on me and I was afraid of what might happen.'

'What sort of effect?' he asked huskily, barely able to force the words out. This was more than he had dared hope for and it was hard to contain his joy.

'One that I never expected to feel.'

She looked him straight in the eyes and he went cold when he saw the anguish on her face. He wanted to tell her to stop then, that he didn't need to know anything else, that he had heard everything that mattered, only he didn't get the chance. The words came out of her mouth and it was as though he had suffered an actual physical blow as they pounded into him.

'I was raped, you see. And that's why I never wanted to feel anything for any man ever again.'

Claire could see the shock on Jude's face and stood up, unable to sit there and watch while shock gave way to anger and then to revulsion. That was what would happen, of course, she thought sickly. Once he got over his initial shock, he would react the way so many other men had done. She had read accounts written by other rape victims describing how their husbands and partners had reacted and they had been remarkably similar: shock came first; anger second; disgust next...

'When did it happen?' His voice grated and she winced. Jude was suffering because he cared about her, because learning what had happened to her hurt *him*. The thought made her feel even worse.

'Just over two years ago.' She plugged in the kettle, not because she wanted a drink but for something to do. She had to hold on to her control and make this as easy as possible for him. The last thing she wanted was him getting hurt.

'Before you went to Mwuranda.'

It was a statement, not a question, and she nodded. 'Yes. That's why I went. I wanted to get away from England.'

'I see. Did you report what had happened to the police?' he continued and she sighed, understanding his need to know all the details. He thought it would help, thought it would make it easier if he filled his head with facts rather than emotions, but she knew better than anyone that nothing could stop the pain.

'No,' she said quietly, hating herself for doing this to him. 'I decided not to go to the police in the end.'

'Because you were afraid of the publicity if the case went to court?'

'That plus the fact that the man who raped me said that nobody would believe me.' She gave a bitter little laugh, stopping abruptly when she heard the note of hysteria that had crept in.

'But that's ridiculous!' Jude leapt to his feet, his eyes blazing with anger. 'Of course they would have believed you, Claire!'

'Maybe.' She gave a tiny shrug. 'And maybe not. I wasn't raped by a stranger, you see. I had been dating this man for a couple of months. That could have made a difference to what the police thought, especially if he'd told them I was trying to get back at him for dumping me.'

'He threatened to do that?'

'Oh, yes.' Her voice caught but she forced herself to carry on. She couldn't break down now. She had to tell Jude everything, every horrible, awful detail. She owed him that. 'The fact that he attacked me because I told him that I didn't want to see him any more was irrelevant. He would have lied if it had meant he would escape punishment.'

'There's no saying the police would have believed him,' Jude said quietly, making an obvious effort to regain control. 'After all, it would have been his word against yours, Claire.'

'True. But he's a lawyer, well respected, apparently, and I wasn't prepared to take that risk.'

She took a quick breath, feeling the foolish tears burning her eyes. She had known how hard it would be to tell him the truth and she should be relieved that it was all out in the open at last. Yet the fear that Jude must view her differently now was unbearably painful. She realised that there was only one thing she could do; she had to make sure he understood that she didn't expect anything from him. Maybe he had said that he loved her but he must feel very differently now that he knew she wasn't the person he had believed her to be, that she was soiled goods, tainted by the past.

'So there you have it. I apologise for misleading you but it seemed the best thing to do.' She held out her hand, her heart aching at the thought of never seeing him again. But it wouldn't be fair to expect him to feel the same about her, to love her, to want her, to spend his life with her. Jude deserved better than her; he deserved a woman who didn't come with such terrible baggage. 'I hope you won't think too badly of me in the future,' she said, her voice breaking.

'And that's it, is it? You've told me the truth and now I'm expected to disappear?' He shook his head, his eyes holding hers fast so that Claire found she couldn't look away. 'Well, I'm sorry to disappoint you but that's not going to happen.'

He took a step towards her. 'You and I could have something really special, Claire. Are you willing to turn your back on that because you're afraid?' Reaching out, he ran the tips of his fingers down her cheek, smiling tenderly when she sucked in her breath. 'Because you do feel something, don't you, Claire? When I touch like this…' he repeated the gentle caress '…you feel the same way I do. Scared, excited, afraid of what's about to happen, afraid that it won't.'

'Jude—' She got no further as he drew her into his arms and cradled her against him.

'It's all right, my love. I understand how scared you must have felt, and how hard it's been for you to deal with what happened to you, but you're not on your own any more. I'm here and I'll always take care of you. You're safe with me.'

His voice was so filled with love that all the doubts which had consumed her suddenly melted away. When his hand moved to her hair and began to stroke it, she nestled against him, loving the feel of his body pressed against her own, so hard and strong and wonderfully reassuring. It struck her then that she had reached a turning point, that never again would she feel scared or ashamed. Telling Jude about the assault had stripped it of its power. Although she would never forget what had happened, she wouldn't let it destroy her life. And it was all thanks to Jude. He had given her back her future.

The thought unleashed all the feelings that she had tried to keep at bay. Reaching up, she drew his head down, kissing him with a passion she had never expected to feel again. But this was different. This was Jude. And he was the man she loved.

Jude gasped when he tasted the hunger on Claire's lips. After what she had told him, he had never expected this! However, there was no denying that she was kissing him as though she really meant it. He kissed her back, letting his lips speak for him. He loved her and he wanted her, and what he had learned hadn't made an iota of difference to any of that. Admittedly, he had been shocked but it hadn't changed his view of her. She was still the most beautiful woman he had ever met, beautiful inside and out too. Nothing that had happened to her in the past—no matter how appalling—would alter how he felt.

The need to tell her that was too strong to resist. He drew back, framing her face between his hands as he looked deep into her eyes. 'I love you, my darling, and I want you to know that what you've told me hasn't made any difference to how I feel about you.'

'Are you sure?' She bit her lip and he could tell

that she was struggling to hold back her tears. 'I'd understand if you felt differently about me, Jude. It must be hard for any man to cope with what I told you, so please don't think that you have to stay with me out of kindness…'

'Kindness has nothing to do with it!' Jude didn't let her finish. He kissed her long and hungrily, wanting to erase any foolish ideas she had about why he wanted to be with her. He loved her so much and the thought of being without her was unbearable.

They were both trembling when they drew apart. Jude ran his knuckles over her swollen lips, filled with awe that she wanted him so much. If he was honest, he didn't feel worthy of her love. He had led such a hedonistic life before they had met, wasted his talents instead of using them to make a difference to people's lives. Surely he should confess all that and make sure she understood exactly what kind of a man he was before they went any further?

Taking her hand, he led her to the sofa, his heart thumping as they sat down. The thought of how she might react when she found out the truth about him wasn't easy to deal with, but it wouldn't be fair to play down his shortcomings after she had been so open with him.

'There's something I must tell you, Claire,' he began.

'It's all right,' she said quickly, her voice catching. 'I understand if you're having second thoughts.'

'I'm not.' He kissed her softly on the mouth then smiled into her eyes. 'Oh, I hate what's happened to you and wish with all my heart that you hadn't had to go through such a terrible ordeal. But it doesn't alter the way I feel about you. How could it when it's part of what has made you the person you are?'

'Are you sure?' She gripped his hand and his heart ached when he felt the tremor that ran through her. 'Sure that it won't make a difference in the future? I couldn't bear that, Jude. Really I couldn't.'

'I'm sure.' He kissed her again then forced himself to pull back before temptation got the better of him. However, he couldn't bear to think that *she* might regret staying with him if she found out about his not-so-glorious past. The thought filled him with dread but he forced himself to continue. 'I think it's only right that you know about my past, Claire. To be honest, I've devoted more time to pleasure than I have to my career in the last few years.'

'That might be true, but you did a brilliant job while you were in Mwuranda,' she protested. 'Everyone said so.'

'Did they? That's good to know.' Jude felt strangely heartened by that news and it helped enormously. 'However, despite those kind words, I know that I could have done an even better job if I hadn't wasted so much time these past five years. To put it bluntly, I've been coasting since I left the NHS.'

'Why did you leave?' she asked quietly, twining her fingers through his as though she sensed how difficult he found it to talk about the reason why he had quit.

'Because I was totally burnt out.' Raising her

hand to his mouth, he gently kissed it. 'I was based at a hospital in the centre of the city and the workload was horrendous. There was never enough staff and we seemed to spend our time playing catch-up—I can't count the number of times we had to cancel a scheduled surgery because there weren't enough qualified staff available. Morale was at rock-bottom, so it wasn't only me who found it hard to cope.' He sighed. 'Despite all that, I probably would have carried on working there if it weren't for Maddie. Her death was the final straw.'

'Was she the child you mentioned when we were looking after Bebe?'

'Yes.' Jude took a deep breath, feeling the pain sear his insides even after all the time that had passed. 'Maddie was one of my patients, thirteen years old and born with a congenital heart problem. She had been in and out of hospital all her life yet, despite that, she was one of the pluckiest, bravest kids I've ever met.' He laughed softly. 'She loved playing tricks on us—you know the sort of thing, whoopee cushions placed on a chair, fake injuries. She just loved having fun.'

'She sounds lovely,' Claire said quietly.

'She was. A lovely, happy child who brought a lot of joy to her family and everyone she came into contact with.'

'What happened to her?' Claire squeezed his hand when he hesitated. 'You don't have to tell me if it's too painful.'

'No, I want to tell you,' he said slowly, realising it was true. Sharing this with Claire would help him put it into perspective, something he had never quite managed to do. 'Maddie was on the heart-lung transplant register as it had reached the point where it was the only option open to her. Anyway, we received notification that organs had become available, so we called her into hospital. She was so excited, not scared, just thrilled at the thought that she'd be able to lead a normal life after the operation.

'Everything was set up and ready, the harvest team was due to arrive and then the unthinkable happened. I had a call from the head of surgery to say that he'd been involved in an RTA on his way in and had broken his wrist. If that wasn't bad enough, he'd had our senior consultant with him, and *he* was suffering from concussion.'

'Oh, no!' Claire exclaimed. 'So what did you do?'

'There was no way we could go ahead with the transplant—we simply didn't have enough staff. As you probably know, time is of the essence in this type of situation. Organs for transplant soon start to deteriorate, so we couldn't wait until we managed to draft in enough staff. I had to contact the transplant team and tell them to offer the organs to another patient. Then I had to tell Maddie.' He lowered his head when he felt tears fill his eyes. 'She was devastated. I think that's when she gave up, because she'd lost all hope of getting better. She died three days later and there wasn't a thing I could do to help her.'

'It wasn't your fault, Jude.' Claire put her arms around him and hugged him. 'You did everything you could.'

'But it wasn't enough to save her.' He hugged

her back, feeling a little better thanks to her closeness. He sighed. 'I handed in my notice the following month and went into the private sector, where I've stayed for the past five years. It's been the easy option, basically. However, it's time I thought about doing more with my life.'

'If it's what you want to do then I'm all for it. But don't do it for the wrong reasons, Jude.' She smiled at him. 'I'll admit that I had my doubts at first. You did seem a bit…well, *full* of yourself. But I soon realised what a superb surgeon you are.'

'Hmm. That's a backhanded compliment if ever I heard one. Full of myself indeed!' He kissed her, taking his time as he lovingly punished her for the comment. Claire sighed when he let her go.

'Sorry, but I did say you were superb at your job, don't forget.' She laughed when he rolled his eyes. 'Anyway, what I'm trying to say is that you shouldn't feel bad about the choices you've made. You needed a break from all the pressure from the sound of it. And as you just told me, your past has made you into the person you are today and I, for one, love every tiny bit of you.'

'That's good enough for me.'

He drew her into his arms, kissing her with a hunger he made no attempt to hide. Claire kissed him back, loving the fact that it felt so right. She had never expected to feel this way and it simply reinforced her decision to put the past behind her. When Jude gently set her away from him, she smiled into his eyes.

'Thank you. I didn't think I would ever feel this happy.'

'Neither did I.' He brushed his lips across her forehead and grimaced. 'I hate to do this but it's time I left. It's late and I'm in Theatre first thing tomorrow morning.'

'Really? I'd have thought you would take some time off before you went back to work,' she queried in surprise.

'I am, but I'm assisting Professor Jackson.' He grinned at her. 'He's agreed to operate on Jeremiah. We managed to get the paperwork all sorted, so we brought him back to England with us.'

'Oh, that's wonderful!' Claire exclaimed.

'Isn't it? However, if I'm to be any help at all then I'd better get some sleep.'

He stood up and Claire got up as well. She took a quick breath to contain the ripple of panic that ran through her. This was a huge step but she was determined to focus on the future and forget the past. 'You don't have to leave. You can stay here, if you like.'

'I'd love to but I don't know if it's a good idea, Claire,' Jude said quietly. Taking her hands, he drew her to him and hugged her. 'I know how difficult it must be for you to think about sleeping with me after what's happened and I don't want you to feel under any pressure. We can wait until you're ready and it doesn't matter how long it takes.'

'Thank you.' She kissed him on the lips, loving him more than ever for being so understanding. 'But I've wasted enough time and now I want to get on with my life, get on with loving you and showing you how much you mean to me.'

'Then why don't we take things really slowly?'

He tipped up her chin and dropped a feather-light kiss on her mouth. 'If I spend the night here, we don't have to make love. We can simply sleep in one another's arms. It sounds wonderful to me. How about you?'

'It sounds wonderful to me too,' she said softly, her heart swelling with happiness at his thoughtfulness.

Jude kissed her again then helped her turn the sofa into a bed. Claire found the pillows and the duvet then hesitated, wondering if she should go and undress in the tiny bathroom.

'Here, let me help you.' Jude took her into his arms and kissed her hungrily before turning his attention to the buttons down the front of her blouse. He worked them free then slipped it off her shoulders and looked at her, studying the ripe curves of her breasts beneath the plain white bra she was wearing. 'You're so beautiful,' he murmured huskily. 'Even more beautiful than I imagined.'

Claire shuddered, more affected than she could say by the thought of him imagining how she looked. When he slid the straps off her shoulders, she stood proudly in front of him, glorying in the fact that he enjoyed looking at her. He didn't see her as soiled goods but as a desirable woman. The woman he loved.

He swiftly dispensed with the rest of her clothes and then it was her turn. Claire's hands were shaking as she grasped the hem of his sweater and drew it over his head. He was naked beneath, his skin deeply tanned underneath a light covering of hair. Reaching out, she ran her palms over the warm strong muscles, savouring the firmness of his flesh, its vitality. She could feel his heart beating beneath her fingertips and closed her eyes, wanting to store away the moment. She didn't feel afraid, as she might have expected. After all, this was the first time she had been intimate with a man since she had been raped. But touching Jude this way felt right; it was what she wanted to do. She knew then that what had happened in the past could no longer hurt her. Love had taken away its power to rule her life.

Jude could feel his desire building but forced

himself to hold back. He didn't want to rush Claire. She needed time and he would give it to her. Tossing back the quilt, he held out his hand, smiling into her eyes when she immediately placed her hand in his. That she trusted him was plain to see and it meant the world to him. He would never betray her trust, he vowed as he drew her down on the bed. No matter what life threw at them, he would always be there for her, would always protect and cherish her until his dying day. She was his present and his future: she was everything to him.

Drawing her into his arms, he kissed her with heart-melting tenderness, feeling the tears running down his cheeks. He couldn't recall ever crying like this before but it didn't matter. He loved her so much that his heart seemed to be brimming over with emotion. When she cupped his face between her hands and began to kiss away his tears, he let her. He wasn't ashamed of her seeing them. If anyone had the right to know how deeply he felt, it was her.

'I love you,' he whispered, holding her close.

'And I love you too. So very much.'

They held each other close, not needing to do or say anything else. They both knew that from this moment on they would be together, that nothing could part them. They might not make love to-night but Jude knew that they would do so soon and that it would be wonderful too. More wonderful than anything they had ever known. They loved each other too much for it to be anything other than perfect.

EPILOGUE

Three years later...

'LADIES AND GENTLEMEN, please join me in welcoming our guest of honour this evening, Dr Jude Slater.'

Claire smiled when everyone started to clap. She knew that Jude had been a little nervous about tonight but he needn't have been. He had become something of a cult figure in the last couple of years as he had expounded his views on poverty in the developing world and what needed to be done about it. A lot of people admired his forthright approach, not least of all her. Jude was making a difference to a lot of people's lives and he deserved all the plaudits that came his way.

She let her mind drift back over what had happened while she listened to his speech. They had been married shortly after his return from

Mwuranda. As Jude had said, there was no reason for them to wait. The service had been held in the church close to her parents' home in Cheshire. All the Worlds Together team had attended, along with her family and friends. It had been a wonderfully happy occasion. As she and Jude had made their vows they had both known that they meant every word. It was the start of their new life together and they wouldn't allow anything that had gone on before to ruin their love for one another.

They had gone to Paris for their honeymoon and it had been everything she had dreamt it would be. They had decided to wait until their honeymoon before they made love. It had been Jude's idea and she had been happy to go along with it, even though she'd had no qualms about how she would feel. In the event, their lovemaking had been everything they had hoped for, the confirmation of their love for one another.

Once they returned to London, she had accepted a senior sister's post at one of the large teaching hospitals while Jude had given up his job in the private sector and set about honing his skills by accepting a post with Professor Jackson's team. His natural talent for surgery had soon made itself apparent and he was much in demand both at home and abroad. However, he had continued to work for Worlds Together and had become a spokesman for them which was what had brought about this invitation to speak at tonight's dinner. They had both found worthwhile careers, although in her case there were to be some changes shortly.

A burst of applause announced that Jude had come to the end of his speech. Claire laughed as he mopped imaginary perspiration from his brow as he came back to their table and sat down. 'Phew! Am I glad that's over!' he declared, leaning over to drop a kiss on her cheek.

'Don't give me that,' she retorted, thinking how handsome he looked in his dinner jacket. 'You know you love the adoration of your fans. I mean, just listen to all that applause!'

'Oh, *please*!' He rolled his eyes. 'They're clapping because I didn't go wittering on for too long.'

'Hmm, if you say so,' she replied, still smiling. She took a quick breath, feeling excitement bubbling up inside her. She had been waiting for this moment all day and now it had arrived at last. 'Talking about fans, you're about to add another one to your club.'

'Am I?' he asked, frowning.

'Yes, you are.' Clare stood up, suddenly deciding that the crowded dining room was not the best place to continue the conversation. 'I'll tell you outside.'

Jude looked puzzled but he got up and followed her from the dining room. She led him across the hotel's foyer to the reading room, which was empty. Closing the door, she turned to look at him, unable to contain her joy a second longer.

'I did a test today while you were practising your speech,' she began, but he cut her off.

'You don't mean—'

'Yes, I do. I'm pregnant! We're having a baby, my darling, which means that in roughly seven months' time there'll be a new little addition to your fan club.'

'Oh, darling!' Jude could barely breathe as a wave of intense joy flooded through him. It was what they had both been hoping for and to finally have it happen was almost more than he could believe. He drew Claire into his arms, realising again how lucky he was. Not only had he found her, his soul-mate, but in a short time he was going to have a son or a daughter too. Life couldn't get any better.

Tilting her face, he looked into her eyes. 'I didn't think it was possible to feel any happier, but it is. I can't tell you how much this means to me, sweetheart.'

'You don't have to because I feel the same.' Taking his hand, she placed it on her stomach. 'We're going to have a baby, Jude. Isn't it wonderful?'

'It is. Completely and utterly wonderful. Just like you.'

He kissed her softly on the mouth, letting his lips tell her just how much this meant to him. He'd thought he was happy before they had met but how wrong he had been. *This* was what true happiness felt like, he thought wonderingly, this feeling of complete and utter bliss. He had found the woman he would love for the rest of his days and they were going to have a child. Nothing could beat this!

* * * * *

If you enjoyed this story, check out these other great reads from Jennifer Taylor

THE GREEK DOCTOR'S SECRET SON
MIRACLE UNDER THE MISTLETOE
BEST FRIEND TO PERFECT BRIDE
ONE MORE NIGHT WITH HER DESERT
PRINCE...

All available now!

MILLS & BOON®
Large Print Medical

May

The Nurse's Christmas Gift	Tina Beckett
The Midwife's Pregnancy Miracle	Kate Hardy
Their First Family Christmas	Alison Roberts
The Nightshift Before Christmas	Annie O'Neil
It Started at Christmas...	Janice Lynn
Unwrapped by the Duke	Amy Ruttan

June

White Christmas for the Single Mum	Susanne Hampton
A Royal Baby for Christmas	Scarlet Wilson
Playboy on Her Christmas List	Carol Marinelli
The Army Doc's Baby Bombshell	Sue MacKay
The Doctor's Sleigh Bell Proposal	Susan Carlisle
Christmas with the Single Dad	Louisa Heaton

July

Falling for Her Wounded Hero	Marion Lennox
The Surgeon's Baby Surprise	Charlotte Hawkes
Santiago's Convenient Fiancée	Annie O'Neil
Alejandro's Sexy Secret	Amy Ruttan
The Doctor's Diamond Proposal	Annie Claydon
Weekend with the Best Man	Leah Martyn

MILLS & BOON®
Large Print Medical

August

Their Meant-to-Be Baby	Caroline Anderson
A Mummy for His Baby	Molly Evans
Rafael's One Night Bombshell	Tina Beckett
Dante's Shock Proposal	Amalie Berlin
A Forever Family for the Army Doc	Meredith Webber
The Nurse and the Single Dad	Dianne Drake

September

Their Secret Royal Baby	Carol Marinelli
Her Hot Highland Doc	Annie O'Neil
His Pregnant Royal Bride	Amy Ruttan
Baby Surprise for the Doctor Prince	Robin Gianna
Resisting Her Army Doc Rival	Sue MacKay
A Month to Marry the Midwife	Fiona McArthur

October

Their One Night Baby	Carol Marinelli
Forbidden to the Playboy Surgeon	Fiona Lowe
A Mother to Make a Family	Emily Forbes
The Nurse's Baby Secret	Janice Lynn
The Boss Who Stole Her Heart	Jennifer Taylor
Reunited by Their Pregnancy Surprise	Louisa Heaton

MILLS & BOON®
Large Print – May 2017

ROMANCE

A Deal for the Di Sione Ring	Jennifer Hayward
The Italian's Pregnant Virgin	Maisey Yates
A Dangerous Taste of Passion	Anne Mather
Bought to Carry His Heir	Jane Porter
Married for the Greek's Convenience	Michelle Smart
Bound by His Desert Diamond	Andie Brock
A Child Claimed by Gold	Rachael Thomas
Her New Year Baby Secret	Jessica Gilmore
Slow Dance with the Best Man	Sophie Pembroke
The Prince's Convenient Proposal	Barbara Hannay
The Tycoon's Reluctant Cinderella	Therese Beharrie

HISTORICAL

The Wedding Game	Christine Merrill
Secrets of the Marriage Bed	Ann Lethbridge
Compromising the Duke's Daughter	Mary Brendan
In Bed with the Viking Warrior	Harper St. George
Married to Her Enemy	Jenni Fletcher

MEDICAL

The Nurse's Christmas Gift	Tina Beckett
The Midwife's Pregnancy Miracle	Kate Hardy
Their First Family Christmas	Alison Roberts
The Nightshift Before Christmas	Annie O'Neil
It Started at Christmas...	Janice Lynn
Unwrapped by the Duke	Amy Ruttan

0417 GEN STD LP